For my father.

Thank you for telling me your stories.

WHAT IT MEANS WHEN A MAN FALLS FROM THE SKY

WHAT IT MEANS WHEN A MAN FALLS FROM THE SKY

LESLEY NNEKA ARIMAH

TINDER
PRESS

The following stories have been previously published,
in slightly different form: 'War Stories' (*Mid-American Review*),
'Light' (*Granta*), 'Second Chances' (*The Butter*), 'Who Will Greet
You at Home' (*The New Yorker*), 'Buchi's Girls' (*Five Points*),
'What It Means When a Man Falls from the Sky' (*Catapult*)

First published by Riverhead, USA

First published in Great Britain in 2017 by Tinder Press
An imprint of HEADLINE PUBLISHING GROUP

1

Cataloguing in Publication Data is available from the British Library

Hardback ISBN 978 1 4722 3961 7

Typeset in 10.4/17.5 pt Berling LT Std by Jouve (UK), Milton Keynes

Printed and bound in Great Britain by
Clays Ltd, St Ives plc

Headline's policy is to use papers that are natural, renewable and recyclable
products and made from wood grown in well-managed forests and other
controlled sources. The logging and manufacturing processes are expected
to conform to the environmental regulations of the country of origin.

HEADLINE PUBLISHING GROUP
An Hachette UK Company
Carmelite House
50 Victoria Embankment
London EC4Y 0DZ

www.tinderpress.co.uk
www.headline.co.uk
www.hachette.co.uk

CONTENTS

▲ ▼ ▲

THE FUTURE
LOOKS GOOD

▲ ▼ ▲

Ezinma fumbles the keys against the lock and
doesn't see what came behind her: Her father as a
boy when he was still tender, vying for his mother's
affection. Her grandmother, overworked to the bone
by the women whose houses she dusted, whose laundry she washed, whose children's asses she scrubbed
clean; overworked by the bones of a husband who
wanted many sons and the men she entertained to give
them to him, sees her son to his thirteenth year with
the perfunction of a nurse and dies in her bed with a
long, weary sigh.

His stepmother regards him as one would a stray
dog that comes by often enough that she knows its

face, but she'll be damned if she'll let him in. They dance around each other, boy waltzing forward with want, woman pirouetting away. She grew up the eldest daughter of too many and knows how the needs of a child can drown out a girl's dreams. The boy sees only the turned back, the dismissal, and the father ignores it all, blinded by the delight of an old man with a young wife still fresh between her legs. This one he won't share. And when the boy is fifteen and returns from the market to find his possessions in two plastic bags on the front doorstep, he doesn't even knock to find out why or to ask where he's supposed to go, but squats with other unmothered boys in an abandoned half-built bungalow where his two best shirts are stolen and he learns to carry his money with him at all times. He begs, he sells scrap metal, he steals, and the third comes so easy to him it becomes his way out. He starts small, with picked pockets and goods snatched from poorly tended market stalls. He learns to pick locks, to hot-wire cars, to finesse his sleight of hand.

When he is twenty-one, the war comes, and while people are cheering in the streets and shouting "Biafra! Biafra!" he begins to stockpile goods. When goods become scarce, he makes his fortune. When food becomes scarce, he raids farms in the dead of night, which is how he will meet his wife, and why Ezinma, fumbling the keys against the lock, doesn't see what came behind her: her mother at age twenty-two, not beautiful, but with the fresh look of a person who has never been hungry.

Her mother is a brash girl who takes more than is offered. It's 1966, months before everything changes, and she is at a party hosted by friends of her parents and there is a man there, yellow skinned like a mango and square jawed and bodied like the statue of David, wealthy; the unmarried women strap on their weaponry (winsome smiles, robust cleavage, accommodating personalities) and go to war over him. When she comes out the victor, she takes it as her due.

Almost a year into their courting, the war comes. Her people are Biafra loyalists, his people think Ojukwu is a fool. On the night of their engagement party only her people attend. And when she goes by his house the next day, she discovers he has left the country.

Her family is soon forced to flee the city, soon forced to barter what they have been able to carry, soon forced to near begging, and for the first time in her life, food is so scarce she slips into farms at night and harvests tender tubes of half-grown corn in stealth.

They boil so soft she eats the inner core and the fibrous husk, too. One night, she finds a small farm tucked behind a hill and there she encounters a man stealing the new yams that would have been hers. There is no competition; he is well fed and strong, and even if she tried to raise an alarm out of spite, he could silence her. But he puts his finger to his lips and gives her a yam. And being who she is, she gestures for two more. He gives her another one and she scurries away. The next night when she returns to the farm, he is waiting for her. She sits by him and they listen to crickets and each other's breathing. When he puts his arm around her, she leans into him and cries for the first time since her engagement party many months ago. When he puts a yam in her lap, she laughs. And when he takes her hand, she thinks, *I am worth three yams*.

She will have two daughters. The first she names Biafra out of spite, as though to say, *Look, Mother, pin your hopes on another fragile thing*. And the second is named after her mother, who has since died and doesn't know that her daughter has forgiven her for choosing the losing side and named her youngest child Ezinma, who fumbles the key against the lock and doesn't see

THE FUTURE LOOKS GOOD

what came behind her: her sister, whom everyone has taken to calling Bibi, because what nonsense to name a child after a country that doesn't exist.

Bibi, who is beautiful in a way her mother never was. Bibi, stubborn like her mother was always. They've fought since Bibi was in the womb, lying so heavy on her mother's cervix a light jog could have jostled her out. Bedridden, Bibi's mother grew to resent her and stewed so hot the child should have boiled in her belly. And three years later, Ezinma, pretty, yes, but in that manageable way that causes little offense. She is a ghost of Bibi, paler in tone and personality, but sweet in the way Bibi can be when Bibi wants something. Bibi loathes her. No, Ezinma can't play with Bibi's toys; no, Ezinma can't walk with Bibi and her friends to school; no, Ezinma can't have a pad, she'll just have to wad up tissues and deal with it. Ezinma grows up yearning for her sister's affection.

When Bibi is twenty-one and her parents are struggling to pay the university fees, she meets Godwin, yellow skinned and square jawed like his father, and falls in love. She falls harder when her mother warns her away. And when her mother presses, saying, You don't know what his people are like, I do, Bibi responds, You're just angry and bitter that I have a better man than you, and her mother slaps her and that's the end of that conversation. Ezinma serves as go-between, a role she's been shanghaied into since her youth, and keeps Bibi apprised of all the family news, despite their mother's demands that Ezinma cut her off.

And Godwin is a better provider than Bibi's father, now a modest trader. He rents her a flat. He lends her a car. He blinds her with a constellation of gifts, things she's never had before, like spending money and orgasms. The one time she brings up marriage, he walks out and she can't reach him for twelve days. Twelve days that put the contents of her bank account in stark relief; twelve days that she sits in the flat that's in his name, drives the car also in his name, and wonders what is so precious about this name he won't give to her. And when he finally returns to see her packing and grabs her hair, pulling, screaming that even this is his, she is struck . . . by his fist, yes, but also by the realization that maybe her mother was right.

The reunion isn't tender. Bibi's right eye is almost swollen shut and her mother's mouth is pressed shut and they neither look at nor speak to each other. Her father, who could never bear the tension between

the two women, the memories of his turbulent childhood brought back, squeezes Bibi's shoulder, then
leaves, and it is that gentle pressure that starts her
tears. Soon she is sobbing and her mother is still
stone-faced, but it is a wet face she turns away so
no one can see. Ezinma takes Bibi to the bathroom, the
one they've shared and fought over since they were old
enough to speak. She sits her on the toilet lid and begins to clean around her bruises. When she is done, it
still looks terrible. When Bibi stands to examine her
face, they are both in the mirror. I still look terrible,
Bibi says. Yes you do, Ezinma replies, and they are
soon laughing, and in their reflection they notice for
the first time that they have the exact same smile.
How have they gone this long without seeing that?
Neither knows. Bibi worries about her things that
are still in the flat. Ezinma says not to worry, she will
get them. Why are you still nice to me? Bibi asks.
Habit, Ezinma says. Bibi thinks about it for a moment
and says something she has never said to her sister.
Thank you.

And so Ezinma fumbles the keys against the lock
and doesn't see what came behind her: Godwin, who
grew up under his father's corrosive indulgence. Godwin, so unused to hearing no it hits him like a wave of

acid, dissolving the superficial decency of a person who always gets his way. Godwin, who broke his cello when he discovered his younger brother could play it better, which is why he came to be here, watching Ezinma—who looks so much like her sister from behind—fumbling the unfamiliar keys against the lock of Bibi's apartment so she doesn't see who comes behind her: Godwin, with a gun he fires into her back.

WAR STORIES

▲ ▼ ▲

This time, my mother and I were fighting about what I had done at school to prove with no question that Anita Okechukwu was not wearing a bra. That Anita and I had been in the middle of the playground hadn't bothered me, that there were boys around hadn't bothered me, but Anita Okechukwu was far more sensitive than I.

"Nwando, you can't just go around opening people's shirts," my mother said after she closed the door on Mrs. Okechukwu, a broad-shouldered, broad-hipped woman whose need for a bra was unassailable. Mrs. Okechukwu had wanted an apology and an explanation, and my mother was ready with the first but unsure of the second. That's why she'd called me onto the veranda to explain myself. I wanted to tell them about how Anita had started the Girl Club after claiming that her father had sent her expensive bras from London edged with barely-there lace and soft ribbons and powdered with fairy dust, and how she made the rule that only girls with bras could be in the Girl Club and that if you weren't in the Girl Club you couldn't sit in the Girl Area and you had to play with the boys. Anita would confirm who was Girl by escorting each applicant behind the school to check if she was wearing the required undergarment. They'd emerge short minutes later, the Bra Princess followed by her newest lady-in-waiting. In the jostling to be a Girl, with friends borrowing one another's intimates and rejected applicants stewing in bitterness, no one had thought to check if Anita actually owned the bras she'd shown us in a catalog.

My mother's raised brow asked, *Well?* and Mrs. Okechukwu frowned at me until my nuanced defense deteriorated into "I wanted to see her bra." My mother pinched her nose and Mrs. Okechukwu muttered about girls with no home training. That's when my mother got angry. I could tell by the way her left shoulder hunched forward with the effort not to make a fist, how her lips pressed so tight they disappeared.

She remained polite to Anita's mother but her glare seared holes into me.

"Wait till your father hears this thing," her cry of last resort. At such moments I became my father's daughter, a confounding creature who had no doubt inherited a vein of insanity from one of his yeye ancestors. I was his problem to solve.

Dinner that night amounted to my mother chewing smugly while I tried to swallow garri around the lump in my throat. My father said nothing.

While my mother cleared the table, he set up the chessboard on the veranda, a sporadic ritual that had begun a few months before, when we relocated to Port Harcourt. As the stand-in for Emmanuel, my father's old friend, I was to match him in chess and swap stories, though my mother drew the line at serving me beer. A poor strategist, I never offered much of a challenge, but my father was a quiet man who did not make friends easily, and I would do.

"So what is this your mother is telling me?" he asked, giving me another chance to explain myself. I had the words this time and told my father about Anita and bras and the machinations of girls. He listened without interrupting, stealing my pawns as I moved them on the board. When I finished, my story dangled in the air between us. Then my father began to tell one of his own.

"When I was your age, my lieutenant—"

"You were in the army when you were twelve?" I interjected, knowing my father's penchant for exaggeration. Emmanuel used to take him to task for it, interrupting my father with laughter and calls for "Truth! Truth!" With Emmanuel gone, the assignment fell to me, but my father didn't crack a smile.

"Lieutenant Ezejiaku was a hard man. I feel bad for him now because he was surrounded by boys and fools and charged with creating an army of men. He would wake us at three in the morning and make us run around the compound with our gear. When we complained, he would shout, 'Do you think the enemy will let you fetch a wheelbarrow to carry your things?' Sometimes he would wake two of us at random in the middle of the night to run drills. We would always fight to sleep in the spots we thought he wouldn't pick."

"Is this about the time he took your gun?"

The tale, intended to impart some inscrutable lesson, was a stale one my father had trotted out at various infractions over my short life. I heard it when I stole lipstick from my aunt's dresser. I heard it when my mother discovered me gathering ants in a plastic bag to put in a schoolmate's hair. I heard it after I got into a fight with the children who said my father was strange, and again when I wanted to know why Emmanuel couldn't come to our house anymore, and later, why he'd done what he'd done. My father never shared stories from before or after the war, as though he'd been born in the barracks and died the night of the final volley.

"Yes, it's about the time he took my gun, and it was entirely my fault. Lieutenant stressed to us time and time again the importance of keeping our weapons within reach and sight at all times. One night, I was eating around the fire and placed my gun behind me. That was when the lieutenant must have taken it. I panicked when I couldn't find my gun, but it never occurred to me that he had it. My friends and I took turns rotating so that when one unit was resting, I would have a weapon. This lasted for three days, until the lieutenant mobilized all the units at once for inspections. When he came to me, he looked me in the eye and handed me my gun. I never sweated so hard in my life."

My father laughed harsh and loud, then quieted,

staring at the chessboard. He was still for so long I wasn't sure if he was contemplating his next move or if this was the genesis of one of the thick skins of silence my mother would spend days peeling off. Just as I was about to go and get her, he moved his queen to check my king and continued.

"I was flogged so hard my back looked like pureed tomatoes. Then they buried me in sand for three days. After that, I never took my eyes off my gun. Checkmate."

I arrived at school the next day a hero. Fellow students patted my back and I was soon surrounded by the girls who hadn't made Anita's club and a few who had but wanted to curry favor with the new regime. By exposing Anita and cutting the head off the beast, I'd inherited my very own Girl Army.

During vocabulary class Ms. Uche asked us to select a word from the dictionary to use in a sentence. The person with the best word would get to lead the class to assembly tomorrow.

"I feel *luminous*," I said, heady with power.

"Stop being *obnoxious*." This from Femi Fashakin,

a thick-waisted girl with a plague of pimples. She'd been part of the Girl Club and wasn't ready to relinquish her membership. Ms. Uche, already bored with the exercise, intervened.

"Why don't we query the class? Class, which word is better, *luminous* or *obnoxious*?"

My army responded like a rehearsed choir.

"*Luminous*!" And Femi Fashakin was put in her place.

Anita Okechukwu fared worse. She hadn't been popular before the supposed bra acquisition, her only claim to fame being that her baby brother was albino, and she couldn't take much credit for that. But she'd tried, and her incessant conversations about a three-year-old earned her a reputation as an odd one. She'd fallen even further now, with girls pointing and laughing at her, which was only to be expected. What I hadn't expected were the boys who ran behind her during recess and lifted up her skirt, as though my actions had given them permission, as though because they had seen her bare breast they were entitled to the rest. It was a boyish expectation most would not outgrow even after they became men.

At first Anita yelled and pulled her skirt down and

chased the offenders, but soon something cracked and though she cried, she no longer tried to stop them. This earned her the reputation of being easy, which would haunt her long past girlhood.

I resisted the urge to walk over to Anita and went instead to the cluster of girls who awaited my command. We sat in a circle looking at each other. I was seated on a crate that had once held soft drinks. Damaris Ndibe, who had installed herself as my second in command, dragged a smaller girl forward and stood her in front of me.

"She lied about the job her older brother got." It took me a minute to realize that I was supposed to set this right somehow. The incident with Anita made me the purveyor of vigilante schoolyard justice, but I'd lost my taste for truth.

I stalled for time.

"What's your brother's name?"

"Emmanuel," she whispered, and though it wasn't *my* Emmanuel, something about the way she said his name, a trigger in her inflection, brought it rushing back. Emmanuel's vigorous laughter, the way he ruffled my hair and pulled up my braids in a bid to make me taller. The way he bartered stories and wit with my father. His growing moroseness, his angry outbursts, the crying that followed. My mother would pull me away from where I eavesdropped and put me to bed. After Emmanuel left, I'd hear them argue, my mother's raised voice saying, "It isn't right, Azike, he isn't right. I don't want him here." But the next week he'd be there again and sometimes he'd be okay and sometimes he wouldn't, and sometimes he'd pull my braids and sometimes he wouldn't, but he was always there. Until he wasn't.

Something pooled in my fist and it itched, then intensified to a stabbing pain I couldn't shake off. I punched the lying girl's nose.

Damaris was the first deserter. She led away the bleeding, shell-shocked girl, sneering over her shoulder. Others followed with rolled eyes and whispered insults. By the end of the day, I was a queen with no pawns.

My mother was livid. This time, there were no half-serious threats to tell my father, no jesting declarations of what incorrigible traits I'd inherited from his line. She spanked me, an undertaking she hadn't performed in years. It was awkward, like running backward.

During dinner, which I wasn't permitted to share with my parents, I sat on a stool in the kitchen, soothing the shrapnel sting on my behind with daydreams of how upset my real parents would be when they discovered these temporary guardians had used me ill. I tried very hard not to think about the little girl and her nose, how it crackled beneath my fist. I tried hard not to think of Emmanuel, how he'd been discovered by the sister with whom he still lived, hanging from the ceiling fan in his bedroom. When I first heard the news, before the full weight of it hit me, I'd wondered out loud if his legs were still kicking, like the chickens whose necks my mother wrung like sodden towels. My mother had given me a strange look. I tried not to think about that.

In the days after Emmanuel's death, my father slipped deeper and deeper into the strangeness that had plagued him his entire life. His growing moroseness, his sudden outbursts of anger or mirth, the deep silences he fell into, so heavy my mother would pry and pry till they fell off. When the chance came for my father to transfer to the Port Harcourt branch of the oil company, my parents had taken it, hoping the distance would help.

This time, my father didn't ask me why I'd done

what I'd done, which was just as well. He laid out the chessboard and we began to play. Every once in a while my mother walked by the door, shoes clipping her anger on the tiles. My father glanced up each time, but I ignored her. He was distracted enough that I was able to maneuver his queen into a precarious position.

He paused, leaned back, and rested his head in cradled hands. The stance was familiar. I knew I was about to hear another of his true war stories.

"We were stationed near a small village around Enugu where the only thing worth seeing was the concrete highway that passed through. During the day it was hot enough to char skin, but at night it cooled. That's when the snakes came out. Dozens of them. They curled on the concrete, which held the sun's warmth late into the night."

He raised and caressed his queen. When my mother again walked by, he was too preoccupied to notice.

"While the snakes slept, Emmanuel would tiptoe to one, slip his rifle through the top of the coil, and shoot off its head. The body flicked around for a couple of minutes, then settled down. Then Emmanuel would bring the snake into our tent to cook it. And the smell, the smell just turned my stomach. He laughed at how queasy I got, but I chose to sleep outside instead of fighting about it."

"I can't imagine that Lieutenant Ezejiaku was too happy with him." I had grown fond of the lieutenant, who I imagined was like a father to my father.

"He didn't really mind until one time when Emmanuel crossed the line. We were walking one evening and there, coiled on the sidewalk, was the biggest snake I had ever seen. I mean, it was bigger around than both of my legs joined together. Emmanuel crept up to it like he always did and fired at the head. The snake went wild. It snapped and flipped so hard, it went off the road and into the bush. Its whipping around even destroyed one of the shacks nearby. Every time it stilled and Emmanuel approached it, the snake sensed him and started flipping around again.

"The next morning, the lieutenant came to our tent and pulled Emmanuel out by his ear. He pointed to a line of villagers who stood not far off. He said, 'They want you. You have been killing their gods and they want me to give you to them for judgment.'"

My father went silent. He took my bishop.

"I had never seen Emmanuel so quiet. He said only one thing: 'Please.' Lieutenant Ezejiaku told him that if one more snake died, he would hand Emmanuel over to the villagers and turn a blind eye to what they did with him. Over the course of the day, a crowd gathered where the snake lay. No one ventured close enough to touch it. Finally, one shirtless boy ran up to it with a stick. His mother screamed at him to get back. He ignored her, the way boys ignore mothers, and poked at the creature. Before we could blink, the snake coiled so tight around the boy, his chest grew purple. He tried to slide the animal off, as one would a pair of too-tight trousers. He was dead in seconds. It took four days before the snake died and they could bury the boy's body."

There was something in my father's eyes, in his voice, as though he hadn't meant to tell this much of the story, as though, perhaps, he had forgotten that this was how it had ended.

"So what happened to the lieutenant?" I asked, wanting another story to erase this one.

"He died, Nwando; they all died."

"How come you didn't die?"

"Because," he said, "when the time came, I ran."

My father dragged at his beer bottle, then focused on the chessboard. The next move was obvious, my queen exposed to his knight and rook. But he didn't move, and I could see that the veil had come over him. My mother, who'd stopped by the doorway to listen, came and gathered me to her. She herded me into my bedroom and sat me down on my bed. I slid under the covers fully dressed. She stroked my head and began to tell me a story of her own, about when she'd been a girl and her cousin found a nest of termites in a tree trunk and the pulp was so syrupy they stirred it like soup. I listened with every atom and she animated the story with everything she had.

WILD

▲ ▼ ▲

Two months before my first semester at Emory—
two months I'd imagined I'd spend getting high in
Leila's basement while we crooned stale power ballads
at each other—my mother sabotaged my summer plans
with a one-way ticket to Lagos and a promise to purchase the return only after I'd earned it. A suitcase was
already packed and my passport, whisked from my
room the week before, was presented to me along with
the ticket, relieving me of excuses. My plane left in
four hours.

"I've just had enough. You can either go and stay
with Auntie Ugo or work at the clinic with me, no
friends, no visits, no nothing. It's up to you, but enough
is enough."

"Enough" had started with stupid teenage things that, magnified under the halo of Chinyere, my well-behaved cousin, made me a bad, bad girl. There was the misfortune of having my first kiss—with Bartholomew Fradkin, who shouldn't even have been in my class but had been held back once in kindergarten, then again in third grade—witnessed by no less than four faculty members and three students. The resulting plague of rumors earned me a lecture from my mother—"You are not like these oyinbo girls, you can't just do your body anyhow"—and an undeserved reputation as a bit of a ho.

"Enough" was the time my mother, looking to treat a headache, found the Ecstasy I'd thought cleverly hidden in an Excedrin bottle, and I came home to her making carpet angels. I joined her and we laughed and laughed till she'd sobered up and the laughing stopped.

Or when I was suspended for calling my Debate and News teacher a fascist cow because she refused to let me argue for abortion rights, an issue I didn't feel one way or the other about until I was denied the option to support it. The suspension lasted a week and a half and that fascist cow scheduled a pop quiz every day I was gone, lowering my GPA by 0.07, enough for Emily Gleason (the fascist cow's niece) to be valedictorian instead of me. When my mother found out, she screamed at me for an hour about responsibility and dedication and all the responsible and dedicated people who had made it possible for me to be here, starting with my great-grandfather, a mere goat herder, who no doubt was curled in his grave, weeping, and ending with my father, God rest his soul.

"You know, they told me to beat you."

"Who?"

"Everybody. They said since you were being raised without a father and in America of all places, if I didn't beat you, you would go wild. And I didn't listen."

"Well, are you going to start now?" My mother was a small woman who carried her weight in her personality. I had three inches and fifteen pounds on her. It would be tricky.

She just shook her head at me, wearing a helpless half sneer that asked whose daughter was this. It was a look I had seen many times.

"I'm sorry?"

"This is because of that girl," she said, ignoring my apology.

"That girl" was Leila, my best friend since the seventh grade. At first our friendship had been one of convenience, a forced camaraderie that came from being the only two nonwhites—and foreigners—in our entire grade. But later that year Leila's mother passed away and, each of us down a parent—mine to a car accident, hers to cancer—we bonded over the loss. My mother had liked Leila at first, preferring that I make friends with other immigrants, but after Leila's mother died and she started acting out, my mother tried to steer me away, although she remained courteous to her.

"There's nothing wrong with Leila. There's nothing wrong with me. There's nothing wrong with anything. We're fine, Mom." My mother threw up her hands and the argument ended as many had before, with her exasperated capitulation.

Or so I thought.

Now, two weeks later, my mother drove to the airport in a silence so heavy it slid across my skin. She'd threatened to send me to my aunt so many times it had become toothless, but the valedictorian thing must have been the last straw. At the airport, she mellowed enough to give careful warnings—don't take anything from strangers, stay at your gate so you don't miss the plane—but I responded in monosyllables, too angry to manage much else.

"Chinyere will be picking you up from the airport. Please be good. I love you."

I could tell right away that I wasn't what she'd expected, this wild American cousin of hers. I was wearing loose jeans, a tank top, and a flannel shirt, which had served in the coolness of the aircraft but I now tied around my waist to circumvent the naija heat. I looked, as always, disappointing. My mother constantly complained about my dressing, the baggy jeans and shirts too masculine for her liking, but I had always dressed for comfort, not much caring how I looked.

Chinyere dressed for style and was much thinner than I'd expected, but without the bony edges that had earned me the nickname "Daddy Longlegs" in my adolescence.

"Chinyere."

"Ada, welcome."

My mother loved invoking Chinyere to nudge me into correct behavior. Chinyere was such a sweet girl; Chinyere went to church, so why couldn't I; Chinyere was so obedient. Even after her indiscretion, the lectures continued. Chinyere was so *nice*, you see, and

called my mother every other Sunday afternoon between three and four, just to chat. There was no
chance of us being friends.

In her car, a sporty but dusty two-door Toyota, my
phone beeped as it connected to a network. Chinyere
held out her hand.

"May I borrow it? Just to make a quick call."

"I don't know, my mom said it would be expensive
and I should buy a phone here and only use this one
for emergencies."

Chinyere didn't push, but the air between us
turned hostile. After a few moments of sitting in traf-
fic, I shrugged and capitulated.

"Here, just make sure it's fast," I said, extending it
to her, but she didn't even look at me.

We were somewhere on the mainland bridge when
she held out her hand again, and this time I gave it to
her. She spoke excitedly to the female voice that answered, telling her to call my number if she wanted
to speak to her and adding that since her cousin was
here, her mother would have to let her go out some-
time, so they could meet up then. After ending the
call, Chinyere explained that her mother didn't allow
her to have a mobile anymore and she wasn't allowed
to go anywhere or do anything.

"I see." This didn't bode well for us having a good time.

At the house, Auntie Ugo rushed out, looking like a wider, taller version of my mother, and hugged me.

"Look at you so grown up. And so tall. You must have gotten that from your father." She said her husband was in Abuja and wouldn't be back till next week, but he was very excited to see me. Then she updated me on people I'd long forgotten, chattering about who was doing what and how proud my mother had been when I got into Emory and how I must be so excited. Not once did she look at Chinyere, who rolled my suitcase behind us.

After a few more minutes catching up, Auntie Ugo went to finish making dinner, pointing me to the guest room upstairs. Along the staircase were pictures of Chinyere as a child, alone, with her parents, with me on the last visit I'd made when I was thirteen. The pictures stopped a couple of years after that, and there were no images of the baby.

In my room, I found Chinyere rifling through my suitcase, pulling out tops and dresses and holding them to her.

"They're all new. Did you go shopping just for this visit?"

I looked at the suitcase. Not a scrap of flannel or denim in sight. No doubt my shirts and jeans were being sorted at a thrift shop right that minute, or possibly aflame in our backyard fire pit.

"Ugh, my mom must have. I don't dress like this." I traced the beaded edge of a black jersey top that managed to accommodate folds and layers and creases. It was so lovely I resented it. "You can have it if you want."

"I have my own clothes."

"Fine."

"Fine."

Auntie Ugo called us.

In the kitchen, she manned several pots while giving instructions to the housekeeper, Madeline, on what to buy, mentioning foods she remembered as my favorites even after all these years. Madeline bounced the baby on her hip and he pulled at her buttons.

"Chi-Chi, why don't you take care of your *brother*," Auntie Ugo said, and the cadence of the request carried the rhythm of one uttered many times. The boy was a year old, bug-eyed and cute. My mother had warned me I was to go along with the pretense in public, but I hadn't expected that even in the privacy of their home we were to act as if the boy wasn't Chinyere's son. Madeline handed him to Chinyere and they both left the room, leaving me alone with my aunt. I didn't know how to fill the silence after her casual malice. She was more than up to it.

"You know, we did everything for that girl, everything. The best schools, the best everything." She tasted the soup and added Maggi, shaking the bottle so vigorously I resigned myself to dinner being a little salty. "But you children, you don't know anything."

She sounded just like my mother, and I knew that if I didn't interrupt, the lecture would escalate until I wanted to slit my wrists just to give her something to mop so she would. Stop. Talking.

"I'm tired," I said.

"Oh, sorry, my dear, go and lie down. Chinyere will get you when the food is ready."

Instead of escaping to the guest room, I went to Chinyere's, where I found her lying on her bed while the boy toddled around waving a comb in the air. She looked up when I walked in, then went back to tempting him with an unlit candle. When he released the comb, she snatched it up and slipped it under her pillow. He grabbed the candle and jabbed the air with it before offering it to me, grinning.

"Don't take it, or he will come looking for the comb again," she said.

The boy grew bored waiting for me to accept his gift and leaned over to tug at the neon-yellow straps of my flip-flops.

"He likes you." She didn't sound like she liked that. Or me.

"What can I say, I have a way with handsome young men. And aren't you handsome? Aren't you deliciously handsome?" The boy squealed and giggled as I picked him up and pretended to snack on his arms and belly. When I stopped, he settled his head into my neck.

"He must be tired," Chinyere said. "Let me take him."

She got up, pulled him out of my arms, and settled him in the hollow of the mattress she'd just vacated. A week ago you couldn't have told me I would enjoy the weight of a child or feel intense satisfaction when he gripped my shirt as his mother removed him. I'd always thought of babies as blobby entities, sometimes powder scented, sometimes poo scented, that I wouldn't need to concern myself with for another decade. But Chinyere had given birth when she was around the age I was now.

"My mom's mad at me too, you know," I said, looking for common ground.

"Her mom"—she imitated my pronunciation, poorly—"gets angry with her and buys her clothes."

"It's not like that."

"Oh? What's it like?"

I didn't feel like explaining—where would I even begin—so I went to my room. I dug through the suitcase looking for anything that was mine, but even the pajamas were new. I picked up the beaded black shirt and put it on. It was as lovely as I'd imagined it would be. I rummaged through my purse and found my phone.

My cousin is a bitch, I typed, then sent to Leila. A few minutes later she responded.

Yeah, I heard your mom sent you back to Africa.
Text me some topless women!

I laughed. Derek Colvin and the guys on the soccer team had taken to calling Leila the Lebanese Lesbian because she refused to date any of them. And being Leila, she sort of ran with it.

This is a $10 text telling you you're an idiot. I don't want to stay here. I'm going to try and guilt my mom into getting me a hotel.

And as though following perfectly timed stage directions, my phone woofed. It was the ringtone I'd programmed for my mother when I was angry with her—a dog barking.

"Hey, Mom."

"Your auntie said you arrived almost an hour ago. You should have called me, or at least texted so I could call you."

"I'm sorry, I just got to catching up with Chinyere and lost track of time."

"That's nice. Maybe she will be a good influence on you."

"Uh, doubt it, what with the baby by her married boyfriend."

My mother paused.

"Single women with children aren't bad people."

I sat up, chastened.

"I'm sorry." Requesting a hotel was out of the question now.

"Did you like my surprise?"

"I'm wearing one of your surprises right now. I look like a whore."

"Chineke, Ada, don't make me choke on my food." She was laughing. "It's just that you are so used to

34

walking around dressed like a boy. You will soon like it."

I hadn't realized how angry I'd been with her until suddenly I wasn't. I wanted to tell her about Auntie Ugo and Chinyere, how it seemed they would come to blows any minute, and how even at our most contentious we had never been like that.

"Thank you."

"Aha, I was waiting for that. I also put a package in there for your auntie Ugo and your uncle. There's some perfume for Chinyere and a little something for the housekeeper. I'm sure your auntie will find you girls something nice to do."

The event my aunt secured us an invitation to was a fund-raiser for a private primary school whose student body consisted mostly of the spawn of the local elite. It was hardly the carousing I had been promised, but it was a way out of the house that met Auntie Ugo's requirement that no one get pregnant. We could only go if we took a phone—mine—and promised to answer it by the second ring. Or else. The invitation promised entertainment and refreshment, and that seemed to be enough for Chinyere. She dressed in a shortish black dress and applied makeup so expertly she looked like a different, glamorous person. I picked a blue dress from the collection my mother had packed and had to admit that when it came to clothing, my mother knew what she was doing. After watching me struggle with a tube of caked mascara, Chinyere went and retrieved an arsenal of tubes and brushes, sat me at the foot of the bed, and went to work. She said nothing except to direct me—close your eyes, smack your lips—and was done not ten minutes after she began. The mirror showed that nice young woman my mother was always hoping for. I looked like a promise fulfilled.

"Can you take a picture for me?" It was all the compliment Chinyere needed on her handiwork, and she smirked as she snapped a picture with my phone. I let her hold on to it, because I didn't like to carry a purse, and I figured she'd want to make another clandestine call once we'd left the house. But she wasn't done with favors.

"You have to do something for me. Ask my mum if we can borrow her car." She rushed over my response. "I used to borrow it all the time, before. I can drive it, I just need you to ask or else she'll say no."

The request seemed harmless enough.

"Okay. But that makes us even."

"Fine."

"Fine."

In the kitchen, Auntie Ugo looked at Chinyere when I asked for the car and continued looking at her as I bullshitted about why it was so crucial—we were dressed so nice, our car should be as nice.

"You are starting again, Chi-Chi? Making people lie for you?" Before Chinyere could respond, Auntie Ugo threw the keys at her. "Oya, take it. But let this be the last time."

Chinyere walked away, leaving me to thank my aunt and rush out before she could utter any last-minute mood-killing pronouncements. In the car, Chinyere leaned her head against the steering wheel of her mother's Mercedes, her knuckles tense where they clutched it. I thought of what it would feel like to have my mother despise me, to have utter disappointment at the center of our relationship. I laid an awkward hand on Chinyere's shoulder and she let me. Then she shook it off. "Let's go." She was smiling now, excited at her release, and I couldn't help catching her mood.

The fund-raiser took place at a convention center

on the island. As we walked in, photographers snapped pictures, directing us to turn this way and that, but Chinyere grabbed my hand before I could stop and shook her head, pulling me to the lobby.

"No one important stops to get their picture taken."

"And we're important?"

"No, but the point is to pretend."

There were a few young women our age, all dressed alike—ushers working the event. The older woman examining invitations rolled her eyes at us, double-checking our invite. We didn't look like we'd be writing any checks.

Our table seated eight people; our chairs were the only empty ones. The woman to our left was dressed in a red that was an unfortunate match to the table-cloth. She smiled at us in that benign nostalgic way older people reserve for the very young. A waiter stopped by our table.

"Red or white?"

Chinyere winked at me and studied the label with a practiced eye.

"Red please, and leave the bottle."

Two glasses in, we were the best of friends. We dug through our complimentary souvenir bags, finding a small clock emblazoned with the school's logo and pamphlets featuring endearing little faces captioned with their plans for the future. Chinyere giggled and pointed out a man two tables over who kept staring at me. Every time I happened to glance at him, his smile grew warmer. At the table next to him a group of older women gathered like birds, dressed in bright shades of traditionals. One stared at Chinyere, but when I told her, she quieted and refused to look in the woman's direction again. When one of our table companions got up a few minutes later, the woman slid into his seat before it could cool.

"Why, Chi-Chi, my dear, I almost couldn't believe it was you. How is your . . . brother?"

Chinyere stiffened. "My brother is fine, he's with my mother."

"And how is she? I'm surprised she didn't come tonight, she really loves these little events, doesn't she?"

When Chinyere didn't respond, she tried a different tack.

"Why don't you stand up and let me see that dress, Chi-Chi, my dear?"

Chinyere hesitated, caught between deference and embarrassment. She stood up and moved to sit right down, but the woman gestured. "Turn around, I want to see the back."

Chinyere hesitated again. This was her mother's battle, not hers, but in the way of these things, she had become collateral damage.

"Why don't *you* turn around?" I said to the woman. "I'd love to describe your outfit to my mother. I didn't know that fabric was still in fashion." The woman looked at me, mouth twitching—amusement or anger, I wasn't sure—then looked back at Chinyere, who had used the distraction to sit down.

The two and a half glasses of wine I'd had swirled in my gut, ready to conjure more impertinence.

"Because I could have sworn I saw a picture of my grandmother wearing that exact outfit. In the sixties."

Someone at the table snorted, but the woman didn't look away from me.

"I am Grace Ogige," the woman said as though I should have known the name. "Who are you?"

"I'm her cousin."

Grace Ogige did some society math in her head— 1 social climber + x = whose mouthy child is this— then smiled.

"Ah, the sister in America. I knew your father, you know. He was a very good friend of mine." A hiccup in her voice suggested more. "He was a godly man from a good family."

I nodded, unsure how to respond. My mother rarely spoke of my father, other than to lecture me about not disappointing him. The woman stared at me for a moment, then scraped a trembling hand under her neckline, her confidence beginning to fray.

"It's too bad he got all mixed up with the wrong type of people. He could have been alive today."

"He died in a car accident. There were no 'wrong type of people.'"

Raised brows around the table echoed what the sane little voice in my head, the one floundering in drink, was trying to tell me: shut up.

"Of course not. It's just funny how he died so quickly, leaving his family's holdings to his wife's relatives. Things just aren't done like that here. I'm sure your mother finds America more comfortable."

She delivered the lines like she'd been waiting for this moment, like she'd rehearsed what she'd say to my mother if they met again. That I was not her made no difference. This was the closest she would get to drawing my mother's blood.

The whole table was silent now, and I regretted taking the heat off Chinyere. Even though my mother had inherited the few properties outside the country, my father's brothers had challenged her right to his businesses in Nigeria, and they had battled it out in the courts for five years, till I was seven. Chinyere's father managed what little my mother had been able to win—the bottle factory, various tracts of land—and wielded some small influence. My father's brothers had retained the majority of his Nigerian holdings, despite the will. The wine began to sour in my belly.

"Well. You two girls enjoy the food. I loaned my chef for the evening, so I know it will be excellent."

I took another foolish sip of wine.

"Yes, well, you've clearly enjoyed your chef."

If possible, the table got quieter.

The woman stared at me for a long minute.

"And what is her son's name?" She nodded at Chinyere.

I was quick to answer, caution dulled by the wine and eager to clap back to the insult I expected to hear.

"Jonathan."

The woman gave us a wide, knowing smile, suspicions confirmed. Her hands still trembled—victory now, or excitement—as she rose and returned to her flock. The other women leaned into her, then stole glances at us, some dabbing their smiles with napkins, others openly snickering.

Chinyere's hand dug so deep into my thigh I was sure she drew blood. Nobody at the table would look at us. I hadn't cried since the time Leila stopped speaking to me for a month after I said I found her annual memorial for her mom a little much. The time before that, I was seven, on the plane that took us away from Nigeria. Half my tears had been imitations of my mother's, and the rest were for friends left behind, soon forgotten. I felt like crying now. Chinyere scraped her chair back, grabbed her purse, and left. I sat, lost. I glanced at the woman who had ruined more than just the evening and she seemed to have moved on, laughing and coyly patting the belly of the man who stood over her, no doubt jesting about the food. Someone touched my hand. The woman in red. She spoke in a low, concerned tone.

"You should probably go after her."

I grabbed the gift bags Chinyere had forgotten.

"Here, take mine too," she said, as though a third clock could turn back the minutes and undo catastrophe.

I thanked her and left, feeling eyes on me but not daring to look around.

In the elevator, my limbs began to shake. I crossed my arms and the trembling moved to my lips. I'd always thought myself so savvy and grown, smoking in Leila's basement, kissing boys in hidden corners, maneuvering my mother with my smart mouth. I'd never felt as much of a child as I did just now.

The elevator opened. A small crowd had gathered in the lobby. Chinyere wasn't among them. As I walked outside, a few photographers mobbed me, waving blurry photos of Chinyere and me that we hadn't posed for. I went over to where we had parked and made two turns around the small lot before realizing that no, I hadn't gotten the spot wrong; the car was gone. Chinyere had left me.

Panic billowed in my belly as I walked back to the event center. Inside, I stopped a young woman in usher red and asked if she had a phone I could borrow. At her cagey expression, I explained my predicament (stranded) without going into the why of it (I'm a walking disaster), and between my American accent and my panic, she must have believed me. She looked to the right and left, then pulled a small phone from her bodice. It wasn't until I had it in my hand that I realized I didn't have any Nigerian numbers memorized. Shit. I dialed my number, hoping Chinyere would answer, but it rang and rang until I was listening to my voice mail asking me to leave a message. I took a deep breath and texted.

> Chinyere, it's Ada, please call this number right
> away, please, I'm so sorry.

I hit send, then remembered what Chinyere would see if she checked more of the messages—My cousin is a bitch and worse—and began to cry.

The usher had returned to her duties but stayed close enough that she could keep an eye on me. I turned away, embarrassed at my sniffling, and leaned on a decorative pillar, my back to the lobby. Then I dialed Leila, who always knew what to do.

"Hello?"

"Hey, it's me, I'm such an idiot; I really fucked up."

"What did you do now?"

I was only a quarter of the way through the condensed version when the phone beeped, then cut off, all the credit used up. The usher, who had been waiting to catch my eye, approached me, smiling softly.

"Did you reach your cousin?"

"Yes," I said, resisting the urge to drag her into the orbit of drama that revolved around me. I handed her the phone, relieved when she slipped it into the front of her dress without seeing the out-of-credit text that had no doubt come through.

I must have looked as awkward as I felt, unmoored, the pillar my only companion, because I kept drawing stares. After a third man nodded and lifted his glass to me, I realized they thought I was a high-class runs girl scoping out her market. I began to see most of the gawking for what it was. *This is a children's fund-raiser,* their looks said, *couldn't this ashewo find somewhere else to lift her skirt?*

I went back outside and stood at the lip of the entrance, just off to the right. Chinyere would come back for me, she wouldn't risk being buried under the avalanche of shit that would shake loose for stranding her visiting cousin in the middle of the night with no way to get home.

The air was muggy and soon a fine dampness settled on my skin. I was partially hidden by a large potted palm, but the electric blue of my dress drew every exiting eye in my direction. Most gave me quick glances before turning to more pressing matters, like studiously ignoring the pushy photographers. But some lingered, and a kindly woman even asked if everything was all right, to which I responded yes, my cousin is coming to get me.

Idleness did what it always did, and I found myself unable to ignore the disquieting information the night had brought me. I'd always believed that any secrets between my mother and me were mostly mine, indiscretions I might confess long after they lost the power to draw her ire. She had always avoided talk of what happened after my father's death and faked cheeriness during what must have been a tumultuous legal battle. What else didn't I know?

The hour grew late and the mad rush of departing guests began to peter out. Even an usher or two had left. I was about to make my way to the parking lot again—maybe Chinyere had returned—when someone tapped my shoulder. It was Chi-Chi's antagonist. She held up one finger to hold off words while she completed a message on her BlackBerry, then looked up.

"You have been standing here all night. Where is Chi-Chi? Don't tell me that girl left you."

I didn't want to hand this woman any more ammunition, but I was also tired, and the long night of rude stares had eaten up a lot of my guilt.

"My driver is coming around, I will take you to your auntie's house."

I didn't dare turn down the offer at this late hour. Besides, it would serve Chinyere right to return and not find me. I followed the woman to the edge of the red carpet, where a gleaming black Range Rover pulled up. A young man stepped out and opened the back door. The woman settled in, then pulled out a bottle of water and sucked at it, the plastic crackling.

She gave the driver directions, which I tried to memorize just in case. Then she watched me till I started to fidget. The wine must not have passed out of my system because I couldn't help myself.

"What?" I said rudely. My mother would have slapped my mouth.

"You look just like him. I didn't see it before, but you do," she said, opening a small tin of Vaseline and moistened her lips. "We were supposed to be married, you know."

My father, a man I had never really thought about, at least not in this way. A man with a past.

"You could easily have been my child. I don't have any girls."

She looked me up and down, lingering at my shoes.

"Your dress is nice."

"My mother picked it."

I hoped the response would hurt her. Instead she laughed.

"You are very clever. You get that from him, too."

She began to ask me questions typical of adults when they're trying to be polite. *How is school? Are you enjoying your trip? How long are you here for?* She followed up with talk of her sons—one my age, two younger. She didn't mention Chinyere. I relaxed, surprised to find myself liking her, this woman who had been my enemy short minutes ago.

It was not long before we pulled up to my aunt's gate. As we waited for the maiguard, she took my chin in her hand and studied my face.

"You are everything I would have expected his child to be."

I wavered between being flattered and being aware that this styled, polished girl was not really me.

"Thank you."

Then the maiguard opened the gate, and we drove through.

Auntie Ugo was on the front steps, dressed in a wrapper and head scarf. No doubt she thought it must be Chinyere and me returning for the night.

I expected their encounter to be hostile and it was,

WHAT IT MEANS WHEN A MAN FALLS FROM THE SKY

but in a different way than I anticipated. My aunt was deferential, calling the woman "ma," while the woman called her Ugo and answered her chattiness with as few words as possible. It was clear she just wanted to leave.

She soon did and Auntie Ugo changed back to her irritated self the moment the gates closed.

"Where is Chinyere?"

"I don't know."

"Does this girl have your phone?"

I nodded.

I expected her to start shouting but she remained calm, putting her cell phone to her ear as she walked into the house.

"Chinyere, my dear, how are you? Are you enjoying yourself?" Her sugary tone should have set off Chinyere's warning bells but I could hear my cousin chattering on the other end.

"And Cousin Ada, is she well?"

More chattering.

"Let me talk to her."

I opened my mouth to say something but my aunt held up her finger and gave me a look of such fury that I shut up.

"Oh, she's in the bathroom? Well, she won't be long I'm sure, I can wait on the line."

More chattering as Chinyere dug a hole deep enough to be buried in.

"She's talking with someone else now? That's a funny something, because Grace Ogige just dropped her off at the house."

The chattering stopped. I imagine Chinyere's heart stopped, too. Auntie put her fury into words now. The intensity of her shouting drove me from the room and traveled up the stairs with me, past the old photos of Chinyere. I stopped in front of the one of us together, arms slung around each other's waists. At thirteen, I'd been taller than her at fifteen, and I remembered her mother teasing her about it.

Through the door to my cousin's room I could see the boy rubbing the sleep from his eyes. I sat on the bed and pulled him into my lap, cradling his head under my chin. He fiddled with the neckline of my dress, then settled. I stroked his head, trying to will the night away. A glance at the clock showed it was past midnight. I wouldn't have blamed Chinyere if she stayed away till morning.

Almost two hours later, I heard the gate creak open

and shifted the boy off me and went to the window. Chinyere came through the gate at a modest, almost penitent pace, as though she'd already begun to beg forgiveness. Auntie Ugo ran up to the car and pulled on the driver's-side door, but Chinyere had locked it, so she started banging on the window, shouting the whole time. I couldn't make out all of the words, but she punctuated each one with a slap to the glass, an unsatisfying substitute for Chinyere's face. My cousin sat in the driver's seat, staring straight ahead. This continued for a good ten minutes. Suddenly Auntie Ugo settled for pointing her finger at the house. I pulled back from the window for a moment in case they looked up and saw me, not that it mattered. Everyone in the neighborhood must have been awake and listening.

Then my aunt resumed her tirade, and I returned to watch. "Don't let me break this window, Chi-Chi. If I break this window, next thing I will break you, do you hear me?"

Chinyere must have believed the threat, because she finally shut off the engine and opened the door. As soon as she did, Auntie Ugo was on her. She held my cousin by a twist at the shoulder of her dress while her free hand went to work. Chinyere absorbed it all, not one finger raised in defense. I pulled away from the window once more. This wasn't a memory I wanted.

The boy was awake again. When he caught me looking at him, he held up his arms, a whine blooming in his throat. The front door slammed and we both jumped. I soothed him before whimper turned to full cry. That's how Chinyere found me, sitting on her bed, her son nestled in my lap.

We were both still in our party clothes, but her dress was torn at the collar. Her makeup was streaked and her tears had irrigated most of it to her neck. She looked like she'd been crying since she left the fundraiser. I couldn't tell how much of her face's puffiness was due to the tears and how much to her mother's open palm.

The boy had begun to bounce when he saw her, twisting to get off my lap. I tried to hold on to him, as Chinyere appeared in no shape to deal with a child.

"Leave him," she said, and the boy waddled over to her. He seemed content to just grip her leg.

"I'm sorry," I said, inadequate as the words felt.

She neither accepted nor rejected the apology but

moved to sit by me, pulling the boy onto her lap. He tried to mush our heads together. Chinyere settled for leaning her head on my shoulder, stiff at first, then relaxing into it. I curled my arm around her. When I felt her tears on my neck, I tightened my grip. The boy touched her face and babbled comfort, the last happy sound we would hear for a while.

LIGHT

▲ ▼ ▲

When Enebeli Okwara sent his girl out in the world, he did not know what the world did to daughters. He did not know how quickly it would wick the dew off her, how she would be returned to him hollowed out, relieved of her better parts.

Before this, they are living in Port Harcourt in a bungalow in the old Ogbonda Layout. The girl's mother is in America reading for a master's in business administration. She has been there for almost three years, in which her eleven-year-old bud of a girl has bloomed. Enebeli and the girl have survived much in her absence, including a stampede at the market that separated them for hours, shoppers fleeing a commotion that turned out to be two warring market women who'd had just about enough of each other's tomatoes. They survived a sex talk, birthed by a careless joke an uncle had made at a wedding, about the bride taking a cup of palm wine to her husband and leaving with a cup of, well, and the girl had questions he might as well answer before she asked someone who could take it as an invitation to demonstrate. They survived the crime scene of the girl's first period, where she proved to be as heavy a bleeder as she was a sleeper, the red seeping all the way through to the other side of the mattress. They survived the girl discovering this would happen every month.

Three long years have passed. Now the girl is fourteen and there is a boy and he is why Enebeli is currently seated on a narrow bench meant for children, in what passes for the lobby of the headmaster's office, a narrow hall painted a blaring glossy white meant to discourage the trailing of dirty child fingers, but let's be serious. The girl is in trouble for sending the boy a note and it is not the first time. Enebeli has seen the boy and, even after putting himself in the shoes of a fourteen-year-old girl, doesn't see the appeal. The boy is a little on the short side. The boy has one ear that is significantly larger than the other. It's noticeable. One can see the difference. Whoever cuts the boy's hair often misses a spot, so that it sticks up in uneven tufts. The only thing that saves the boy from Enebeli is that he seems as confused about the girl's attention as everyone else.

The headmaster calls Enebeli in and hands him the note. This one reads, "Buki, I love you. I will give you many sons," and it takes everything Enebeli has not to guffaw. Where does the girl get all this? Not from her mother, whose personality and humor are of a quieter sort, and not from him, who would be perfectly content sitting by a river, watching the water swirl by. He promises to chastise the girl, assures the headmaster that it will not happen again. It happens two more times before the girl learns to pass notes better. And he should chastise the girl, he knows that, but she is his brightest ember and he would not have her dimmed.

The girl's mother attempts to correct the girl, but much is lost in transmission over the wires, and her long absence has diluted much of the influence a mother should have. It is one of the things Enebeli and his wife disagree on, this training up of the girl, and it has widened the schism between them.

The first month wife and mother had gone to the States, the family called and spoke to each other several times a day. The mother and girl would have their time, full of tears and *I miss you*s, and the husband and wife would have their time, full of tears and *I miss you*s as well, but full of other things too, like *my body misses you* and *all I need is thirty minutes max* and *when are you coming home.*

She'd returned the first long holiday, Christmas. Enebeli memorized her scent and the feel of her hair. He'd often find himself staring at her. They slept very little, making up for lost time. When her return to the States was fraught with delays and visa issues, they made their first big mistake, deciding that she should not risk traveling back to Nigeria again for the duration of her studies. There was some noise made about how the girl should accompany her mother—she had barely left her side the whole visit—but Enebeli vetoed it and his wife relented. They knew that of the two of them, she might be able to soldier on without her daughter, but Enebeli would shrivel like a parched plant.

So the girl stayed with him and they learned to survive, but for one relationship to thrive, the other must not, and Enebeli saw this dwindling in the conversations the girl had with her mother via Skype. They were friendly conversations, filled with the exchanging of news and the updating of situations, but there was a whiff of distance, as though the girl was talking to her favorite aunt whom she loved very much but would not, say, tell about a boy.

At fourteen the girl is almost a woman, but still a girl, and her mother is trying to prepare her for the world. Stop laughing so loud, dear. How is it that I can hear you chewing all the way here in America? What do you mean Daddy made you breakfast, you are old enough to be cooking. Distance between mother and daughter widens till the girl doesn't enjoy talking to her mother anymore, begins to see it as a chore.

And speaking of chores, father and daughter share them, each somewhat inept, each too intimidated by their sullen house girl to order her around. She spends most of the day watching Africa Magic, mopping the same patch of tile till it gleams, and when she isn't pretending to clean, the house girl talks to the girl in whispers and Enebeli isn't concerned because they are in the house and how much trouble could they get into. Talk is just talk. This is what he tells his wife, but his wife is horrified and worried that the girl is learning all the wrong ways to be in the world and she badgers and badgers till Enebeli sends the house girl back to her village. The girl becomes sullen with her mother after this and waits with arms crossed for the Skype calls to end, and the mother becomes more nitpicky, troubled that her daughter cannot see she is trying to ease her passage. What is this the girl is wearing? The girl should be sitting with her legs crossed at the ankles. Why is the girl's hair scattered like that, when was the last time she had a relaxer?

Enebeli shrugs at the hair questions and his wife sighs, then says she's calling her sister. Enebeli balks at this. His wife's sister is a terrifyingly competent woman with three polished, obedient sons and the wherewithal to take on another child. She's been trying to get her hands on the girl for years. In a fit of spite and panic, Enebeli buys a box of relaxer and does the girl's hair himself, massaging the cream into her scalp like lotion, and the smell of it makes both their eyes water. When they wash it out, half the girl's hair comes out with it, feathery clumps that swirl into the drain like fuzzy fish.

His wife's sister doesn't say a word about the over-processed mess, or about the scab forming on the girl's forehead, but when she brings the girl back, her hair is shorn close to her scalp, and she turns her head this way and that, preening, and they all, even her mother, agree that her skull has quite the lovely shape and, yes, she looks beautiful. But then her mother ruins it by adding that she can't wait till it grows out so she can look like a proper girl again. This starts another argument between husband and wife, mild at first, but then it peppers and there is this thing that distance does where it subtracts warmth and context and history and each finds that they're arguing with a stranger.

The girl stops talking to her mother, and for a week his wife pleads with him to soften her and he agrees. But really he enjoys having the girl like this, as angry with her mother as he is, and so he does nothing. It doesn't matter; the girl holds a grudge as well as she holds water in her fist, and soon she is chattering away. But the space between mother and daughter has widened to hold something cautious, an elephant of mistrust and awkwardness. The girl feels it, doesn't want it, and in a bid to close the distance, confesses to her mother about the boy. She strings his virtues out like Christmas lights—he's shorter than her, so he has to obey her, he's finally learning how to kiss well—and her mother silences her by saying, sadly, that she didn't think she'd raised that kind of girl. This is the first time the girl becomes aware that the world requires something other than what she is. It dampens her for a few days that worry Enebeli, and then she returns, but there is a little less light to her.

And when his wife says that she has been offered a job in the States, management at a small investment firm, Enebeli says nothing. They promised each other at the beginning of all this that when she got her degree, she would come back and find a snazzy job as a returnee where she would be overcompensated for her foreign papers.

Later, even knowing what it will do to him, she will request that he send the girl to her in America, where her mothering hand will be steadier. He will fight her. He will use vicious words he didn't know he had in him, as though a part of him knows that his daughter will never be this girl again.

But before all this, before the elders are called in, before even his own father sides with his wife, and his only unexpected ally is his wife's sister. Before he bows to the pressure of three generations on his back. Before he sobs publicly in the Murtala Muhammed airport, cries that shake his body and draw concern and offers of water from passersby. Before he spends his evenings in the girl's room, sitting with the other things she left behind, counting down the time difference till they can Skype. Before she returns from school and appears on his screen more subdued than he's ever seen her. Before he tries to animate her with stories of the lovelorn boy who keeps asking after her. Before she looks offscreen as though for coaching and responds, *Please, Daddy, don't talk to me like that.* Before she grows cautious under the mothering of a woman who loves but cannot comprehend her. Before she quiets in a country that rewards her brand of boldness, in her black of body, with an incredulous fascination that makes her put it away. Before all that, she is eleven and Enebeli and the girl sit on the steps to the house watching people walk by their ramshackle gate. They are playing azigo and whenever the girl makes a good move she crows in a very unladylike way and yells, *In your face!* and he laughs every time. He does not yet wonder where she gets this, this streak of fire. He only knows that it keeps the wolves of the world at bay and he must never let it die out.

SECOND CHANCES

▲ ▼ ▲

Ignore for a moment that two years out of grad school I'm old enough to buy my own bed and shouldn't ask my father to chip in on a mattress, so that he shows up with my mother, who looks like she's stepped out of a photograph, and she tries to charm the salesman, something she was never good at, but it somehow works this time and he takes off 20 percent. Ignore for a moment that she is wearing an outfit I haven't seen in eighteen years, not since Nigeria, when she was pregnant with my younger sister, though not yet showing, and fell down the concrete steps to our house, ripping the dress from hem to thigh. Ignore that she flits from bed to bed, bouncing on each one like she hasn't sat on a mattress in a while, and the salesman follows her around like he'd like to crawl in with her. Ignore all this because my mother has been dead for eight years.

My father avoids the look I give him and I'm glad there are beds around because I collapse onto one, unable to stand. When I grab my father's wrist—I cannot at this juncture imagine touching *her*—he twists away from me. I follow him but he refuses to be cornered, so I walk up to my mother and ask, "What the hell are you doing here?"

The salesman looks at me like I kicked her and my mother looks pained, like I might as well have. But shock leaves very little room for guilt.

"Your daddy and I are buying you a bed, didn't you say you wanted a bed?"

The gentle chiding is something I never thought I'd hear again and my knees almost buckle, but something about the casual way she's correcting me, like she's got any right, angers me.

"Why are you here? You're supposed to be—"

My father interrupts this. "Do you want the bed or not?"

Both of them stare at me expectantly. I want to press the issue, but I also really, really need the bed. I nod and the salesman hesitates like he doesn't want to give the discount if it's for me, then walks away to ring it up. My mother is digging through her purse and I know it's not to pay because she never does when my dad is around. But maybe she's different now. Then she sighs and says, "Ike, darling, have you seen my sunglasses?"

The photo my mother has stepped out of was taken in 1982. She is wearing a green ankara-print caftan belted at the waist and it billows becomingly. There is a red patina on the photo that has developed over time. As she stands in the kitchen now, humming as she checks the cupboards, I see that the red tint is on her, starker against the white of the cabinets than at the store. The edges of her face are soft, as though she's kept the slight blur of the photo as well. Slung over her shoulder is the tan raffia purse. All that's missing are her red sunglasses. In the picture, they are tucked into the V at her neck, awaiting the Enugu sun. My father putters around her, and he is grayer, paunchier, slower than the last time I saw them together, but they move the same way, a tender, familiar dance. Every time I take a breath to say something, my father glances at me and his delight shuts me up.

When they bend their heads together and begin to whisper, I slip away from the counter and into my father's room. I have to find the photo.

It's missing from the dressing table that, even after all this time, still holds my mother's jewelry and perfumes, glittering bottles that range from Avon to Armani. The jewelry is just as varied, but most of it is costume, loud, baubly pieces crusted with bling. My mother wore no jewelry in the photo, not even a ring, as she and my father weren't wed at the time but brave young lovers with, as my mother used to say, nothing to prove. There are other pictures of her on the dressing table. One when she was a child, stiff between her parents, long dead. Pictures of her at my high school graduation, on my dad's fiftieth birthday, and my favorite, the one where she's fluffing my baby sister's frilly white pantaloons and my dad snaps just when Udoma kisses the top of Mom's head. Udoma. I hear the front door open and she calls out in that Lucy-I'm-home way of hers and I rush to warn her before it's too late.

When Udoma walks in, she pauses for a stunned moment and my father holds his arms out like *ta-da!* and she does what I should have done when I first saw my mother: she runs to her and holds her so tight about the waist it's a wonder Mom can breathe, her sobs shaking them both.

There's no way I'm going back to my apartment. I call in to work and leave a message punctuated by unconvincing coughs. It's my thirteenth strike, but I don't care. Udoma is practically in Mom's lap, telling her every stupid thing she's ever wanted to tell her and then some. Like my dad, she has simply accepted my mother's presence like it's nothing. I sit off to the side while the three of them are pressed close. Udoma stops and stares at Mom's face and I wait for her to say something about it, but she just moves to the floor and snuggles her head into Mom's stomach. She was ten when our mother died and just off the plane from Lagos for summer vacation. She's filling Mom in on that trip and then on every trip after that, eight years of miles. My dad occasionally interrupts to update my mother on who is where now, and it is the first time he acknowledges that she's been gone.

"And what about you, Uche, what have you been doing?"

They wait to see if I'll play along.

"I've been getting over you. You know, because you're dead."

My mother puts her hand to her chest, where the sunglasses should be, like I've just cursed, and my father shakes his head.

As the silence grows, I leave.

I was a child prone to hysterics. Every cut was a deep wound that would surely keloid and scar me for life, every playground slight an unforgivable infraction that merited a meltdown. I also took to stealing, a habit that saw me disinvited from many of my schoolmates' homes, so that I spent most of my free time playing in the salon/furniture shop my mother ran. I often wonder if I turned out the way I did from all those hours of inhaling turpentine and hair spray. When things were slow, my mother and her assistant, Obiageli, would curl my hair into elaborate dos. There exists a picture of me grinning as though showing off all my teeth would save the world, hair curled and fanned around my head like gele. Obiageli had persuaded my mother to powder my face, aided by my accompanying tantrum that'd worn down her reluctance. I resemble a Texas debutant turned trophy wife flanked by my exhausted-looking mother, because above all else, I was exhausting. My father was posted in Algiers by the oil company he worked for, and many times, until Udoma, it was just my mother and me. My childhood hysterics eventually congealed into an off-putting self-centeredness that was the topic of my mother's and my last conversation, eight years ago.

After my mother died, I spent a few months in a place where they spooned food and medication into me. My father and I have never spoken of the state he found me in, Alabama, to which I had run away, home to The Ex I'd promised never to see again. Nor have we spoken of the state he found me in, catatonic after a handful of pills, curled in a moon of vomit. But when I came to, I was in a hospital and he was there and I just knew things had to get better. I was twenty-two.

It had taken me a year and a half to get my shit together and then five years to complete a master's in technical communications that should have taken two. I'd lived at home until a year ago. But after years of feeling like an exposed nerve, I'd finally myelinated. I still had trouble holding a job and worked the parts table at a pipe supply a few days a week. Sometimes even those few days would be too much and I'd disappear. But those absences became less frequent as things got better and I began to be a person again. And now she just shows up, la-dee-dah ho-hum, like it's not a big fucking deal.

I resume my search for the photograph. I avoid my old room, still the cyclone of a mess I left it in. If it's in there, it will never be found. I head to Udoma's instead, where it's neat as a catalog. I start with the closest chest of drawers, as uncluttered as the room, every sock and panty folded into a tidy square. It's easy to see that the picture isn't here. I reach my hand into the drawer and scatter her things anyway. I'm moving on to the next drawer when Udoma sighs in the doorway. I ignore her and continue digging. I can feel it coming upon me, the unfurling of myself until all that will remain is a raw center. I have to find the picture. I have to.

Udoma stills me with a hand on my shoulder. She hugs me from behind and I am once again taken by her intuition. It was like that growing up, too, starting after we moved to Houston when she was only five and I was seventeen. She's always been able to sense my mood, what it needs, and contort herself to fit that need. Now she whispers: "Why can't you let me have this? Please let me have this."

But I can't.

"She's supposed to be *dead*."

Udoma flinches at the word.

"Don't you have questions?"

"I don't care. You shouldn't care either. You were so unhappy when she . . . left. How can you be upset that she's back?"

I face her. She is dressed in the uniform required by the Christian high school she attends. I've never asked her if she really believes, wary of introducing yet another complication into my story—adding unbeliever! and sinner! to psycho!—but she's always seemed so sure about everything, so accommodating of fate in a way that eludes me. I envy her that sureness. I envy her the uncomplicated relationship with our mother, where Mom was just Mom and not yet a woman with whom she disagreed. I retreat to avoid answering and run into my mother in the doorway.

"Have you girls seen my sunglasses?"

My answer to Udoma's question has sucked the moisture from my throat and I move past her, unable to speak. Udoma murmurs something and my mother murmurs a reply and they no doubt begin a touching conversation I will never be a part of.

Downstairs, my father has fallen asleep on the couch, a glass of wine and his cell phone on the table in front of him. I wonder what my mother said when he poured it, as he's been a teetotaler since before I was born. He looks larger than I've ever seen him, as though inflated with glee, and he snores loudly, the soundtrack of my youth. I notice it then, a grimy white corner peeking out of his phone case from a slot meant to house credit cards. I lift the case and run to the small guest bathroom, locking myself inside. I grip the white corner and slide it out.

The photo has been folded, then folded again, so that it accordions open to reveal a red-tinged couch and the edge of a large speaker that serves as an end table. My mother, who should be standing in front of the couch, is missing. In the corner, so small I almost miss them, are the sunglasses she searches for, almost off frame.

A sob gurgles in my throat. I sit to steady myself and my right leg bounces a nervous jig. I remember our last conversation.

I was in the living room, waiting till it was time to

pick up Udoma from the airport. She'd spent two summer months with my aunt, whom I disliked for her utter disinclination to put up with my bullshit. It was close to time for me to leave and I just kept flipping through TV channels till I fell asleep.

I woke to my mother's yelling. "You mean you are still here? I get a call from the airport police because they think your sister is abandoned, and you are here? I thought something happened to you!"

Her urgency chased away the grogginess and I was suddenly alert and apologetic. A quick glance showed that I was almost four hours late and panic flowered in my stomach. I knew my mother was beyond common fury because she tossed her Bible on the couch like it was a dime-store novel. She shoved her phone in my face, the one she turned silent every Wednesday night so that she didn't get distracted at Bible study, and there were almost thirty messages. I had violated her cardinal immigrant rule: Live quietly and above the law.

"Every time, Uche, every time I ask you to do a simple thing you cannot do it."

"I'm sorry."

"You're sorry, you're sorry. Always sorry. No." She cut my response off at the knees. "What you are is disappointing. You are so disappointing. You are

WHAT IT MEANS WHEN A MAN FALLS FROM THE SKY

disappointing." The last iteration was said not with calcifying anger but an abrupt sadness that under-scored the truth of it. In that timbre resonated my every fuckup. Every tantrum I'd pulled, every item I'd stolen, every time she must have cringed at having to introduce me as her daughter.

I ran out to the patio and slammed the door so hard it cracked, the sound of splintering glass taking the edge off my hurt. My mother started up again, shout-ing as she grabbed her keys and went to pick up Udoma.

I never told my father about our last exchanged words, nor Udoma. Not even the therapist at that place who dug and dug because he knew I kept some-thing from him. The secret of it settled a cloak of guilt on me I will wear for the rest of my life.

Now, when no frantic knocks sound, I begin to feel the sheepishness of a child who has hidden whom no one cares to find. I emerge to see my father where I left him, oblivious to the missing photograph. Someone has put a blanket on him. The clang of kissing pots comes from the kitchen and I know who is there. She glances up at me when I enter but returns to the task at hand, a bouquet of ingredients to turn into soup.

"Why won't you let yourself enjoy this?" my mother

says, and it echoes Udoma's *Why can't you let me have this* so closely I suspect a conspiracy. When I say nothing, she turns to me, naked hen in hand, and asks a question whose answer has thorned my side.

"Nnwam, what do you want from me?"

I want you to boil the chicken with onions and salt. I want you to melt the palm oil on medium heat and sizzle ogbono till it dissolves. I want you to cough when the pepper tickles your throat. I want you to sprinkle in crayfish so tiny I believed, at age four, they'd been harvested half-formed from their mother's womb. I want you to watch the ogbono thicken the water and add the stockfish and the okra and the spinach and the boiled meat and the salt you never put enough of and call us when it's ready and say grace and be gracious and forgive me.

The answer I give: the lopsided shrug I manage when I can't find words.

She turns back to chopping and I leave when the onion gets to her eyes. When I enter my room, I try to conjure happier memories, but all that comes to mind is five minutes ago and the last time we spoke. I crawl into my old bed, still half covered in items I promised to sort, and hug a skein of yarn to my chest, hoping for the temporary erasure of sleep.

She is gone in the morning. The kitchen holds her remains, a turned-over pot in the dish rack and the scent of okra. I find my father on the couch, showered and dressed. His eyes are red and swollen, but he is smiling. Udoma sleeps on the settee close by. They must have spent the night talking.

My father checks the slot on his phone case and sighs, like he never expected the picture to still be there. The picture. It should be in the pocket I frantically pat, then turn inside out. I run to my room and check the bed, tossing aside wool and books and purses long out of style. When I can't find it, I tear the sheets off, sending everything to the floor. Then I see the photograph, almost unrecognizable for the crumpled state it's in. I try to smooth it out, but it's almost torn in two, my mother's face split open in a paper imitation of the accident's aftermath. I unravel to those many years ago, to Alabama, and only now can I utter the words that have haunted me.

"I'm sorry. I love you. Please forgive me."

WINDFALLS

▲ ▼ ▲

The first time you fell, you were six. Before then, you were too young to fall and had to be dropped, pushed, made to slip for the sake of authenticity. You learned to fall out of self-preservation as your mother pushed too hard, dropped from too high a height. You have been living off these falls for years, sometimes hers, but mostly yours. A sobbing child garners more sympathy than a pretty but aging mother of one.

There is a science to it, falling. One can't just trip over one's own foot, land on one's face, and expect a payoff. First, find (or create) a puddle of some sort. Pierce one or two shrink-wrapped containers of chicken and discreetly allow the draining fluid to pool on the floor. When the fall begins, think of it as a dance: right leg up (two, three, four), left leg buckle (two, three, four), land askew, and await the attention of an audience. Cry silent tears at first that build to anguished wails as all efforts to remain stoic come to naught. Have one's child cry along for effect, or better yet, drop her during the fall, let her slip off the hip. As an added bonus, her injuries will be real.

Every year, approximately six hundred lawsuits are filed against grocery stores and supermarkets across the nation due to negligence, discrimination, coupon infringement, etc. Two hundred of these cases are dismissed without fanfare, one hundred are battled out in court, but the remaining three hundred are settled for undisclosed amounts and gag orders. The odds are in your favor.

You haven't always lived this way, or so you imagine. There is a well-preserved, wallet-sized family portrait your mother carries in her purse that shows her sitting down with a baby (presumably you) in her lap. She is younger and prettier, wearing a "mom" sweater she'd never be caught dead in now, crazily patterned and hued, as though designed by an epileptic in the full swing of seizure. Standing behind her is a man, that "ugly sonofabitch" who fathered you and then died two and a half years later, blown to so much fleshy debris in an offshore accident. All you remember of him are his hands, large and hairy, and the metallic taste of the thick gold ring he always wore. In that same purse, your mother carries a picture of the house she bought with the settlement she was awarded after the accident. The house is beautiful. This is the picture she clutches when she cries.

Your mother is a woman who craves the attention of men. After the money came, so did they, poking their way into her life and her bank account, draining both. The settlement money was gone by the time you were four, as was the house, put up as collateral for some pretty-boy venture. Something about a gym or a tanning salon, you don't remember which. It's not something you talk about.

You like to believe that the first fall, the one that left you with a permanent brace on your ankle, was real. That she was reaching over to grab the biggest, freshest eggplant off the display but slipped and, oh shit, dropped the baby. The store settled without a fuss, blaming the overzealous produce misters for leaving the floor wet. The money lasted for a good three years, and would probably have lasted longer were it not for

Matthias, the auto mechanic. And Chuks, the bouncer. And Dwayne, the sex offender, as you soon found out. Some people find it easy to be good when the going is good but lack the fortitude for hardship. Your mother is among them.

She could have gone to her father, head bowed so low she'd have gravel and leaves in her hair, but she'd married against his wishes, moved to the States against his wishes, and had you against his wishes, all with a man he called "that fool from Calabar." The extended family had been forbidden to attend the wedding, and you have no idea what your grandfather looks like except that you look nothing like him and your mother is grateful for this.

You've changed names and addresses so many times that you've written "Amara" on dusty cars across the country and in coffee grounds spilled on motel breakfast counters, you whisper it as you fall asleep, so you don't forget which name is real. And so it goes, year after year: the fall, the payoff, the glitz. Always followed by slipping out of apartment windows and rented trailers, clothing stuffed in pillowcases and grocery bags thrown into the trunk of the car (please, God, let it start), and on to the next town, the next mark.

———

You were sitting in the lobby of Jones and Margus, cradling your arm, which was in a cast. It may as well have been Hunter and Cleb, or Dynasty and Associates, any in the string of ambulance-chasing firms you had used in the past. Your mother was beside you and pulled you up when you were motioned into a small office. In firms this size, a junior associate, some hapless new graduate from an area law school, screens plaintiffs.

You were relieved to see a woman behind the desk. This spared your mother the embarrassing last resort of offering a blow job to convince the lawyer to take your case. (It also relieved you of extending one yourself, discreetly of course—and only after you'd turned thirteen—when your mother excused herself on a false trip to the bathroom.) As the woman rattled off the information you'd provided so far, you picked up a letter opener resting on the edge of the desk and twirled it between your fingers. The handle was weighty and appeared to be carved from bone.

"I am sorry, but I don't think we'll be able to move forward with your case." You were prepared for this, and your mother launched into a diatribe. It was tearful and ugly and manufactured, right down to the last sniffle. The clerk sat there, polite but unmoved, watching you instead of your mother. You realized your mistake, that you should have been the one with the tearful monologue this time. It's a tricky thing, this act.

If one is working with a child, use her on the women. Most will have children of their own, others will wish they did, so tears are guaranteed to elicit concern. Women should work on the men themselves, breasts a-heavin', tears a-flowin'. When age leeches tautness from face and body, take note as men's eyes follow the child's ripening form. For a brief span of years, she will be perfect: old enough to capture men's lust, young enough to rouse women's sympathy. Make use of this.

"Marsha will see you out, and I'll need that back, please," the associate said, indicating the letter opener you still had in your hand. As you were handing it back to her, handle first, you looked into her eyes. They were knowing, like she saw through you. You felt as though you were falling and you don't know what got into you, but you didn't let go. It became a tug-of-war that the associate eventually won, but only by jerking the letter opener out of your hand at an angle that sliced into your palm.

Your mother, ever the opportunist, screeched, "Oh my God, you cut her! Oh, baby, Graceline, are you okay? I'm pressing charges!"

The woman apologized profusely, wadding up tissue to stanch the trickle of blood. But your mother was in full swing by then, the bleeding palm her prop, and launched into the lobby with you in her grip.

The firm exchanged a large check for dropped charges and your silence, and for months you lived like queens. You moved into a motel where you had your own bed, a rarity, and your mother gave you a daily allowance to spend at the fairgrounds a quarter mile away. You hobbled to the grounds while your mother occupied herself with shopping and the men who darted in and out of her life like a lizard's tongue. You spent the days balancing on the Ejection Seat and testing your aim at the Chump-a-Lump. You insisted on riding the Tunnel of Love by yourself, despite the efforts of Giles, the carnie, to find you a partner ("C'mon, fellas, you aren't going to let the little lady go by herself") and his efforts to join you later at night when he clocked out. The children who waited in line giggled at you for riding alone. While they spent their day at the fair dodging overbearing parents and piles of manure from the livestock on display, you, too much your mother's daughter in face and body, dodged the hands of eager men.

"Baby, I'm so proud of you."

Your mother lay next to you on your bed and picked at the plastic fittings on your brace, a nervous habit she'd gotten from you. The scent of Chinese food wafted from the trash in the corner, where the roaches that never bothered her would soon gather. She waved her hand, heavy with costume rings, at the room. "All this because of you." Your palm, marred with a hoary scar, itched.

You never considered another lifestyle, tethered to your mother by familiarity and a notion of loyalty. Then you discovered your pregnancy. You were sitting in the parking lot of a 7-Eleven when your mother handed you a five-dollar bill to purchase tampons, something she'd been doing with soldierly regularity the third week of every month since you'd turned twelve.

"I'm surprised you haven't asked me yet."

In the silence that followed, the words weighed heavy. You ended up purchasing a pregnancy test instead, and thirty-five minutes later, under the flickering fluorescent of a gas station bathroom, the fetal presence was confirmed.

There were a few paternal options. One was Billy, the law clerk and recipient of a blow job that had gotten out of hand. Upon catching you, your mother had flashed your birth certificate, verifying the delivery of a baby girl now fifteen and too young to be bent over that desk, bare stomach resting on the polished wood, servicing a man almost twice her age. He'd wasted no time sliding your suit to the top of the pile. The money had lasted a few weeks, until you had to pay for your car to be towed off the highway to the Lucky Leaf Truck Stop. There you were assisted by Randall the trucker, who turned out to be the guy a girl had to do to get a ride around here. He'd let you out three days and two thousand miles later, leaving you with one last blast of his horn and a wad that amounted to $850. You used this money to purchase a car from Jerry, the used-car salesman, who had to be persuaded to discount the price of the dark green Camry that had caught your mother's eye.

You couldn't afford to see a doctor and rarely

settled in a town long enough to locate the free clinic, so you spent every spare dollar on baby books, parenting manuals, and potty-training tomes. You were convinced you could change a diaper in 12.8 seconds.

"'Very young children require stability as they grow to ensure sound development,'" you read out loud from your latest acquisition, *Formula for a Well Child*. Your mother was watching the road. You were six months along and had begun hinting to her that your unstable life wouldn't "contribute a fair environment" for the baby. "What do you think about that?"

She turned up the radio, cutting you off. A deep, thrumming bass filled the car. She ignored you often now, getting up to leave when you were on one of your "baby rants," as she called them. But at the moment you were captives of a moving vehicle, so you decided to press the issue and twirled the volume low.

"We can't keep doing this. We need to stop, *really* stop somewhere."

"You think I'm stupid or something? I know we got to stop somewhere."

"Okay, but it needs to be soon." You patted your belly, now the dimensions of one of those personal-sized watermelons. Earlier, you'd speculated to your mother that it could be twins, but she'd just rolled her eyes. You grabbed the side of the door as the car swerved to the shoulder. Your mother rounded on you.

"If you've got something to say, say it."

"I'm just saying it needs to be soon. If you're going to stop, it needs to be soon, that's all."

"Why, you think I don't know these things? You think I'm a bad mother or something?"

The question came from left field. Was she a bad mother? You were fifteen years old and pregnant because she wanted a price cut on a battered green Toyota. You weren't sure how to answer, so you didn't. She pulled back onto the road and continued, silent.

At the next town she stopped at the first grocery store you saw. You'd insisted on eating as healthy as you could manage and made frequent stops for fruit, which you ate hastily to avoid rot. Your mother pulled into the furthest open parking spot and handed you a twenty.

"Hurry up." She levered her seat back and closed her eyes.

You eased out of the car and made your way to the store. Right outside, a group of girls with signs identifying them as Glyndon Elementary School students were selling cookies to exiting customers. Two women, probably moms to some of the girls, stood watch behind them, making change and straightening uniforms. One woman, short and round like a grapefruit, adjusted a girl's ponytail. The girl bobbed her head as she spoke and the ponytail came out lopsided and loose; the woman would have to redo it soon. It was a simple, effortless act but you realized that you'd never felt your mother's hands in your hair in quite that way. You continued past them into the store and picked up a shopping basket. Instead of heading for the grocery aisle, you began to look for the section that stocked children's clothing. You wouldn't buy anything until you found out the sex of the child and there was money to spare, but it was nice to look.

A group of small boys barreled toward you, ice-cream cones in hand. "Excuse me, ma'am," "'Scuse me," "Sorry." They politely avoided slamming into you and you smiled after them, which was why you didn't see the puddle of melting ice cream one boy left behind.

You dropped the shopping basket. Your feet slid out from under you, right crossing behind left. The metal edges of the brace failed to find purchase on the tile. Your knee buckled and you put your hands out to catch your weight. Your face angled forward. You knew from years of practice that your chin would be the point of impact and you braced yourself. But your belly caught your fall. It held, then crumpled and spread like a ball of Play-Doh under a child's fist. The pain was instant and blinding. You heard someone wailing and the concerned murmur of the crowd that gathered. When the keening of an ambulance sounded in the distance you blacked out.

You lost the baby. The nurse informed you as soon as you woke. She was brisk and added, "You're young yet." It was a girl, and you thought about the pink bib you'd passed up two towns ago. You wavered in and out of consciousness as your body shut down to repair itself. You weren't allowed any visitors for several hours. The first was your mother, unsurprisingly.

It was the middle of the day, but your lids were still heavy. You lay on your side, a recommendation from the doctor. The curtains were drawn shut and the dim light lulled you back to sleep. You woke every few minutes as your mother entered and exited the room. You could hear her voice in the hallway. It was shrill, and you knew she was either excited or angry. She walked in and took a seat. Her hand stroked your sweaty head and she leaned into you, lips rubbing your ear as she whispered.

"Five hundred *thousand* dollars, baby. That's my girl."

You pulled your head out from under her hand. She smoothed the sheets across your shoulders and to anyone looking at that moment she must have resembled a concerned caretaker. Maybe if you continue looking at her from that angle, you'll begin to believe that too.

WHO WILL GREET
YOU AT HOME

▲ ▼ ▲

The yarn baby lasted a good month, emitting dry, cotton-soft gurgles and pooping little balls of lint, before Ogechi snagged its thigh on a nail and it unraveled as she continued walking, mistaking the little huffs for the beginnings of hunger, not the cries of an infant being undone. By the time she noticed, it was too late, the leg a tangle of fiber, and she pulled the string the rest of the way to end it, rather than have the infant grow up maimed. If she was to mother a child, to mute and subdue and fold away parts of herself, the child had to be perfect.

Yarn had been a foolish choice, she knew, the stuff

for women of leisure, who could cradle wool in the comfort of their own cars and in secure houses devoid of loose nails. Not for an assistant hairdresser who took danfo to work if she had money, walked if she didn't, and lived in an "apartment" that amounted to a room she could clear in three large steps. Women like her had to form their children out of sturdier, more practical material if they were to withstand the dents and scrapes that came with a life like hers. Her mother had formed her from mud and twigs and wrapped her limbs tightly with leaves, like moin-moin: pedestrian items that had produced a pedestrian girl. Ogechi was determined that her child would be a thing of whimsy, soft and pretty, tender and worthy of love. But first, she had to go to work.

She brushed her short choppy hair and pulled on one of her two dresses. Her next child would have thirty dresses, she decided, and hair so long it would take hours to braid and she would complain about it to anyone who would listen, all the while exuding smug pride.

Ogechi treated herself to a bus ride, only to regret it. Two basket weavers sat in the back row with woven raffia babies in their laps. One had plain raffia streaked with blues and greens, while the other's baby was entirely red, and every passenger admired them. They would grow up to be tough and bright and skillful.

The children were not yet alive, so the passengers sang the call-and-response that custom dictated:

Where are you going?
I am going home.

Who will greet you at home?
My mother will greet me.

What will your mother do?
My mother will bless me and my child.

It was a joyous occasion in a young woman's life when her mother blessed life into her child. The two girls flushed and smiled with pleasure when another woman commended their handiwork (such tight lovely stitches) and wished them well. Ogechi wished them death by drowning, though not out loud. The congratulating woman turned to her, eager to spread her admiration, but once she had looked Ogechi over, seen the threadbare dress, the empty lap, and the entirety of her unremarkable package, she just gave an embarrassed smile and studied her fingers. Ogechi stared at her for the rest of the ride, hoping to make her uncomfortable.

When Ogechi had taken her first baby, a pillowy thing made of cotton tufts, to her mother, the older woman had guffawed, blowing out so much air she should have fainted. She'd then taken the molded form from Ogechi, gripped it under its armpits, and pulled it in half.

"This thing will grow fat and useless," she'd said. "You need something with strong limbs that can plow and haul and scrub. Soft children with hard lives go mad or die young. Bring me a child with edges and I will bless it and you can raise it however you like."

When Ogechi had instead brought her mother a paper child woven from the prettiest wrapping paper she'd been able to scavenge, her mother, laughing the whole time, had plunged it into the mop bucket until it softened and fell apart. Ogechi had slapped her and her mother had slapped her back, and slapped her again and again till their neighbors heard the commotion and pulled the two women apart. Ogechi ran away that night and vowed never to return to her mother's house.

At her stop, Ogechi alighted and picked her way through the crowded street until she reached Mama Said Hair Emporium, where she worked. Mama also owned the store next door, an eatery to some, but to others, like Ogechi, a place where the owner would bless the babies of motherless girls. For a fee. And Ogechi still owed that fee for the yarn child who was now unraveled.

When she stepped into the Emporium, the other assistant hairdressers noticed her empty arms and snickered. They'd warned her about the yarn, hadn't they? Ogechi refused to let the sting of tears in her eyes manifest and grabbed the closest broom.

Soon, clients trickled in, and the other girls washed and prepped their hair for Mama while Ogechi swept up the hair shed from scalps and wigs and weaves. Mama arrived just as the first customer had begun to lose patience and soothed her with compliments. She noted Ogechi's empty arms with a resigned shake of her head and went to work, curling, sewing, perming until the women were satisfied or in too much of a hurry to care.

Shortly after three, the two younger assistants left together, avoiding eye contact with Ogechi but smirking as if they knew what came next. Mama dismissed the remaining customer and stroked a display wig, waiting.

"Mama, I—"

"Where is the money?"

It was a routine Mama refused to skip. She knew perfectly well that Ogechi didn't have any money. Ogechi lived in one of Mama's buildings, where she paid in rent almost all of the meager salary she earned, and ate only once a day, at Mama's next-door eatery.

"I don't have it."

"Well, what will you give me instead?"

Ogechi knew better than to suggest something.

"Mama, what do you want?"

"I want just a bit more of your joy, Ogechi."

The woman had already taken most of her empathy, so that she found herself spitting in the palms of beggars. She'd started on joy the last time, agreeing to bless the yarn baby only if Ogechi siphoned a bit, just a dab, to her. All that empathy and joy and who knows what else Mama took from her and the other desperate girls who visited her back room kept her blessing active long past when it should have faded. Ogechi tried to think of it as an even trade, a little bit of her life for her child's life. Anything but go back to her own mother and her practical demands.

"Yes, Mama, you can have it."

Mama touched Ogechi's shoulder and she felt a little bit sad, but nothing she wouldn't shake off in a few days. It was a fair trade.

"Why don't you finish up in here while I check on the food?"

Mama had not been gone for three minutes when a young woman walked in. She was stunning, with long natural hair and delicate fingers and skin as smooth and clear as fine chocolate. And in her hands was something that Ogechi wouldn't have believed existed if she hadn't seen it with her own eyes. The baby was porcelain, with a smooth glazed face wearing a precious smirk. It wore a frilly white dress and frilly socks and soft-soled shoes that would never touch the ground. Only a very wealthy and lucky woman would be able to keep such a delicate thing unbroken for the full year it would take before the child became flesh.

"We are looking for this Mama woman. Is this her place?"

Ogechi collected herself enough to direct the girl next door, then fell into a fit of jealous tears. Such a baby would never be hers. Even the raffia children of that morning seemed like dirty sponges meant to soak up misfortune when compared with the china child to whom misfortune would never stick. If Ogechi's mother had seen the child, she would have laughed at how ridiculous such a baby would be, what constant coddling she would need. It would never occur to her that mud daughters needed coddling, too.

Where would Ogechi get her hands on such beautiful material? The only things here were the glossy magazines that advertised the latest styles; empty product bottles, which Mama would fill with scented water and try to sell; and hair. Hair everywhere, short, long, fake, real, obsidian black, delusional blond, bright, bright red. Ogechi upended the bag she'd swept the hair into and it landed in a pile studded with debris. She grabbed a handful and shook off the dirt. Would she dare?

After plugging one of the sinks, she poured in half a cup of Mama's most expensive shampoo. When the basin was filled with water and frothy with foam, she plunged the hair into it and began to scrub. She filled the sink twice more until the water was clear. Then she soaked the bundle in the matching conditioner, rinsed, and toweled it dry. Next, she gathered up the silky strands and began to wind them.

Round and round until the ball of hair became a body and nubs became arms, fingers. The strands tangled together to become nearly impenetrable. This baby would not snag and unravel. This baby would not dissolve in water or rain or in nail polish remover, as the plastic baby had that time. This was not a sugar-and-spice child to be swarmed by ants and disintegrate into syrup in less than a day. This was no practice baby formed of mud that she would toss in a drain miles away from her home.

She wrapped it in a head scarf and went to find Mama. The beautiful woman and her beautiful baby had concluded their business. Mama sat in her room counting out a boggling sum of money. Only after she was done did she wave Ogechi forward.

"Another one?"

"Yes, Mama."

Ogechi did not uncover the child and Mama didn't

WHAT IT MEANS WHEN A MAN FALLS FROM THE SKY

ask, long since bored of the girl's antics. They sang the traditional song:

> Where are you going?
> *I am going home.*
>
> Who will greet you at home?
> *My mother will greet me.*
>
> What will your mother do?
> *My mother will bless me and my child.*

Mama continued with her own special verse:

> What does Mama need to bless this child?
> *Mama needs whatever I have.*
>
> What do you have?
> *I have no money.*
>
> What do you have?
> *I have no goods.*
>
> What do you have?
> *I have a full heart.*
>
> What does Mama need to bless this child?
> *Mama needs a full heart.*

Then Mama blessed her and the baby and, in lieu of a celebratory feast, gave Ogechi one free meat pie. Then she took a little bit more of Ogechi's joy.

There was good reason for Ogechi not to lift the cloth and let Mama see the child. For one, it was made of items found in Mama's store and even though they were trash, Mama would add this to her ledger of debts. Second, everybody knew how risky it was to make a child out of hair, infused with the identity of the person who had shed it. But a child of many hairs? Forbidden.

But the baby was glossy, and the red streaks glinted just so in the light and it was sturdy enough to last a full year, easy. And after that year she would take it to her mother and throw it (not "it" the baby, but the idea of it) in her mother's face. She kept the baby covered even on the bus, where people gave her coy glances and someone tried to sing the song, but Ogechi stared ahead and did not respond to her call.

The sidewalk leading to the exterior door of her little room was so dirty, she tiptoed along it, thinking that if her landlord weren't Mama, she would complain.

In her room, she laid the baby on an old pillow in

an orphaned drawer. In the morning, it would come to life, and in a year it would be a strong and pretty thing.

There was an old tale about hair children: Long ago, girls would collect their sheddings every day until they had a bundle large enough to spin a child. One day, a storm blew through the town and every bundle was swept from its hiding place into the middle of the market, where the hairs became entangled and matted together. The young women tried desperately to separate their own hairs from the others'. The elder mothers were amused at the girls' histrionics, how they argued over the silkiest patches and longest strands. They settled the commotion thus: every girl would draw out one strand from every bundle until they all had an equal share. Some grumbled, some rejoiced, but all complied, and each went home with an identical roll.

When the time came for the babies to be blessed, all the girls came forward, each bundle arriving at the required thickness at the same time. There was an enormous celebration of this once-in-an-age event and tearful mothers blessed their tearful daughters' children to life.

The next morning, all the new mothers were gone. Some with no sign, others reduced to piles of bones stripped clean, others' bones not so clean. But that was just an old tale.

The baby was awake in the morning, crying dry sounds, like stalks of wheat rubbing together. Ogechi ran to it, and smiled when the fibrous, eyeless face turned to her.

"Hello, child. I am your mother."

But still it cried, hungry. Ogechi tried to feed it the detergent she'd given to the yarn one, but it passed through the baby as if through a sieve. Even though she knew it wouldn't work, she tried the sugar water she had given to the candy child, with the same result. She cradled the child, the scritch of its cries grating her ears, and as she drew a deep breath of exasperation, her nose filled with the scent of Mama's expensive shampoo and conditioner, answering her question.

"You are going to be an expensive baby, aren't you?" Ogechi said, with no heat. A child that cost much brought much.

Ogechi swaddled it, ripping her second dress into strips that she wound around the baby's torso and limbs until it was almost fully covered, save for where Ogechi imagined the nose and mouth to be. She tried to make do with her own shampoo for now, which was about as luxurious as the bottom of a slow drain, but the baby refused it. Only when Ogechi strapped the child to her back did she find out what it wanted. The baby wriggled upward and Ogechi hauled it higher, then higher still, until it settled its head on the back of her neck. Then she felt it, the gentle suckling at her nape as the child drew the tangled buds of her hair into its mouth. Ahh, now, this she could manage.

Ogechi decided to walk today, unsure of how to nurse the child on the bus and still keep it secret, but she dreaded the busy intersection she would cross as she neared Mama's Emporium. The people milling about with curious eyes, the beggars scanning and calculating the worth of passersby. Someone would notice, ask.

But as she reached the crossing, not one person looked at her. They were all gathered in a crowd staring at something that was blocked from Ogechi's sight by the press of bodies. After watching a woman try and fail to haul herself onto the low-hanging roof of a nearby building for a better view, Ogechi pulled herself up in one, albeit labored, move. Mud girls were good for something. She ignored the woman stretching her arm out for assistance and stood up to see what had drawn the crowd.

A girl stood with her mother, and though Ogechi could not hear them from where she perched, the stance, the working of their mouths, all was familiar. They were revealing a child in public? In the middle of the day? Even a girl like her knew how terribly vulgar this was. It was no wonder the crowd had gathered. Only a child of some magnitude would be unwrapped in public this way. What was this one, gold? No, the woman and the girl were not dressed finely enough for that. Their clothes were no better than Ogechi's.

The child startled Ogechi when it moved. What she'd thought an obscene ruffle on the front of the girl's dress was in fact the baby, no more than interlocking twigs and sticks—was that grass?—bound with old cloth. Scraps. A rubbish baby. It cried, the friction sound so frantic and dry, Ogechi imagined a fire flickering from the child's mouth. A hiccup interrupted the noise and when it resumed it was a human cry. The girl's mother laughed and danced, and the girl just cried, pressing the baby to her breast. They uncovered the child together, shucking a thick skin of cloth and sticks, and Ogechi leaned as far as she could without falling from the roof to see what special attribute might have required a public showing.

The crowd was as disappointed as she was. It was just an ordinary child with an ordinary face. They started to disperse, some throwing insults at the two mothers and the baby they held between them for wasting everybody's time. Others congratulated them with enthusiasm—it was a baby after all. Something didn't add up, though, and Ogechi was reluctant to leave until she understood what nagged her about the scene.

It was the new mother's face. The child was as plain as pap, but the mother's face was full of wonder. One would think the baby had been spun from silk. One would think the baby was speckled with diamonds. One would think the baby was loved. Mother cradled mother, who cradled child, a tangle of ordinary limbs of ordinary women.

There has to be more than this for me, Ogechi thought.

At the shop, the two young assistants prepped their stations and rolled their eyes at the sight of

Ogechi and the live child strapped to her back. Custom forced politeness from them and with gritted teeth they sang:

Welcome to the new mother.
I am welcomed.

Welcome to the new child.
The child is welcomed.

May her days be longer than the breasts of an old mother and fuller than the stomach of a rich man.

The second the words were out, they went back to work, as though the song were a sneeze to be excused and forgotten. Until, that is, they took in Ogechi's self-satisfied air, so different from the anxiousness that had followed in her wake whenever she had had a child blessed in the past. The two girls were forced into deference, stepping aside as Ogechi swept where they would have stood still a mere day ago. When Mama walked in, she paused, sensing the shift of power in the room, but it was nothing to her. She was still the head. What matter if one toenail argued with the other? She eyed the bundle on Ogechi's back but didn't look closer and wouldn't, as long as the child didn't interfere with the work and, by extension, her coin.

Ogechi was grateful for the child's silence, even though the suction on her neck built up over the day to become an unrelenting ache. She tired easily, as if the child were drawing energy from her. Whenever she tried to ease a finger between her nape and the child's mouth, the sucking would quicken, so she learned to leave it alone. At the end of the day, Mama stopped her with a hand on her shoulder.

"So you are happy with this one."

"Yes, Mama."

"Can I have a bit of that happiness?"

Ogechi knew better than to deny her outright.

"What can I have in exchange?"

Mama laughed and let her go.

When Ogechi dislodged the child at the end of the day, she found a raw, weeping patch on her nape where the child had sucked her bald. On the ride home, she slipped to the back of the bus, careful to cradle the child's face against her ear so that no one could see it. The baby immediately latched on to her sideburn and Ogechi spent the journey like that, the baby sucking an ache into her head. At home, she sheared off a small patch of hair and fed the child, who took the cottony clumps like a sponge absorbing water. Then it slept, and Ogechi slept, too.

If Mama wondered at Ogechi's sudden ambition, she said nothing. Ogechi volunteered to trim ends. She volunteered to unclog the sink. She kept the store so clean, a rumor started that the building was to be sold. She discovered that the child disliked fake hair and would spit it out. Dirty hair was best, flavored with the person from whose head it had fallen. Ogechi managed a steady stream of food for the baby, but it required more and more as each day passed. All the hair she gathered at work would be gone by the next morning and Ogechi had no choice but to strap the child to her back and allow it to chaw on her dwindling nape.

Mama was not curious about the baby, but the two assistants were. When Ogechi denied their request for a viewing, their sudden deference returned to malice tenfold. They made extra messes, strewing hair after Ogechi had cleaned, knocking bottles of shampoo over until Mama twisted their ears for wasting merchandise. One of the girls, the short one with the nasty scar on her arm, grew bolder, attempting to snatch the cover off the baby's head and laughing and running away when Ogechi reacted. Evading her became exhausting, and Ogechi took to hiding the child in the shop on the days she opened, squeezing it in among the wigs or behind a shelf of unopened shampoos, and the thwarted girl grew petulant, bored, then gave up.

One day, while the child was nestled among the wigs and Ogechi, the other assistants, and Mama were having lunch at the eatery next door, a woman stopped by their table to speak to Mama.

"Greetings."

"I am greeted," Mama said. "What is it you want?"

Mama was usually more welcoming to her customers, but this woman owed money, and Mama subtracted each owed coin from her pleasantries.

"Mama, I have come to pay my debt."

"Is that so? This is the third time you have come to pay your debt and yet we are still here."

"I have the money, Mama."

"Let me see."

The woman pulled a pouch from the front of her dress and counted out the money owed. As soon as the notes crossed her palm, Mama was all smiles.

"Ahh, a woman of her word. My dear, sit. You are looking a little rough today. Why don't we get you some hair?"

The woman was too stunned by Mama's kindness to heed the insult. Mama shooed one of the other assistants toward the shop, naming a wig the girl should bring. A wig that was near where Ogechi had stashed the baby.

"I'll get it, Mama," Ogechi said, standing up, but a swift slap to her face sat her back down.

"Was anyone talking to you, Ogechi?" Mama asked.

She knew better than to reply.

The assistant Mama had addressed snickered on her way out and the other one smiled into her plate. Ogechi twisted her fingers into the hem of her dress and tried to slow her breathing. Maybe if she was the first to speak to the girl when she returned, she could beg her. Or bribe her. Anything to keep her baby secret.

But the girl didn't return. After a while, the woman who had paid her debt became restless and stood to leave. Mama's tone was muted fury.

"Sit. Wait." To Ogechi, "Go and get the wig and tell that girl that if I see her again I will have her heart." Mama wasn't accustomed to being disobeyed.

Ogechi hurried to the shop expecting to find the girl agape at the sight of her strange, fibrous child. But the girl wasn't there. The wig she'd been asked to bring was on the floor, and there, on the ledge where it had been, was her baby. Ogechi pushed it behind another wig and ran the first wig back to Mama, who insisted that the woman take it. Then Mama charged her, holding out her hand for payment. The woman hesitated but paid. Mama gave nothing for free.

The assistant did not return to the Emporium, and Ogechi worried that she'd gone to call some elder mothers for counsel. But no one stormed the shop, and when Ogechi stepped outside after closing, there was no mob gathered to dispense judgment. The second assistant left as soon as Mama permitted her to, calling for the first one over and over. Ogechi retrieved the baby and went home.

In her room, Ogechi tried to feed the child, but the hair rolled off its face. She tried again, selecting the strands and clumps it usually favored, but it rejected them all.

"What do you want?" Ogechi asked. "Isn't this hair good enough for you?" This was said with no malice, and she leaned in to kiss the baby's belly. It was warm, and Ogechi drew back from the unexpected heat.

"What have you got there?" she asked, a rhetorical question to which she did not expect an answer. But then the baby laughed, and Ogechi recognized the sound. It was the snicker she heard whenever she tripped over discarded towels or dropped the broom with her clumsy hands. It was the snicker she'd heard when Mama cracked her across the face at the eatery.

Ogechi distanced herself even more, and the child struggled to watch her, eventually rolling onto its side. It stilled when she stilled, and so Ogechi stopped moving, even after a whir of snores signaled the child's sleep.

Should she call for help? Or tell Mama? Help from whom? Tell Mama what, exactly? Ogechi weighed her options till sleep weighed her lids. Soon, too soon, it was morning.

The baby was crying, hungry. Ogechi neared it with caution. When it saw her, the texture of its cry softened and—Ogechi couldn't help it—she softened, too. It was hers, wasn't it? For better or for ill, the child was hers. She tried feeding it the hairs again, but it refused them. It did, however, nip hard at

Ogechi's fingers, startling her. She hadn't given it any teeth.

She wanted more than anything to leave the child in her room, but the strangeness of its cries might draw attention. She bundled it up, trembling at the warmth of its belly. It latched on to her nape with a powerful suction that blurred her vision. *This is the sort of thing a mother should do for her child,* Ogechi told herself, resisting the urge to yank the baby off her neck. *A mother should give all of herself to her child, even if it requires the marrow in her bones. Especially a child like this, strong and sleek and shimmering.*

After a few minutes, the sucking eased to something manageable, the child sated.

At the Emporium, Ogechi kept the child with her, worried that it would cry if she removed it. Besides, the brash assistant who had tried to uncover the child was no longer at the shop and Ogechi knew that she would never return. The other assistant was red-eyed and sniffling, unable to stop even after Mama gave her dirty looks. By lockup, Ogechi's head was throbbing and she trembled with exhaustion. She wanted

to get home and pry the baby off her. She was antici-
pating the relief of that when the remaining assistant
said, "Why have you not asked after her?"

"Who?" *Stupid answer*, she thought as soon as she
uttered it.

"What do you mean who? My cousin that disappeared, why haven't you wondered where she is? Even
Mama has been asking people about her."

"I didn't know you were cousins."

The girl recognized Ogechi's evasion.

"You know what happened to her, don't you? What
did you do?"

The answer came out before Ogechi could stop it.

"The same thing I will do to you," she said, and the
assistant took a step back, then another, before turning
to run. At home, Ogechi put the child to bed and
stared until it slept. She felt its belly, which was cool-
ing now, and recoiled at the thought of what could be
inside. Then it gasped a little hairy gasp from its little
hairy mouth and Ogechi felt again a mother's love.

The next morning, it was Ogechi's turn to open
the store and she went in early to bathe the baby

with Mama's fine shampoo, sudsing its textured face, avoiding the bite of that hungry, hungry mouth. She was in the middle of rinsing off the child when the other assistant entered. She retreated in fear at first, but then she took it all in—Ogechi at the sink, Mama's prized shampoo on the ledge, suds covering mother-knows-what—and she turned sly, running outside and shouting for Mama. Knowing that there was no use calling after her, Ogechi quickly wrapped the baby back up in her old torn-up dress, knocking over the shampoo in her haste. That was when Mama walked in.

"I hear you are washing something in my sink." Mama looked at the spilled bottle, then back at Ogechi. "You are doing your laundry in my place?"

"I'm sorry, Mama."

"How sorry are you, Ogechi, my dear?" Mama said, calculating. "Are you sorry enough to give me some of that happiness? So that we can forget all this?" There was no need for a song now as there was no child to be blessed. Mama simply stretched her hand forward and held on, but what she thought was Ogechi's shoulder was the head of the swaddled child.

Mama fell to the ground in undignified shudders.

Her eyes rolled, as if she were trying to see everything at once. Ogechi fled. She ran all the way home, and even through her panic, she registered the heat of the child in her arms, like the just-stoked embers of a fire. In her room, she threw the child into its bed, expecting to see whorls of burned flesh on her arms but finding none. She studied the baby, but it didn't look any different. It was still a dense tangle of dark fiber with the occasional streak of red. She didn't touch it, even when the mother in her urged her to. At any moment, Mama would show up with her goons, and Ogechi was too frightened to think of much else. But Mama didn't appear, and she fell asleep waiting for the pounding at her door.

Ogechi woke in the middle of the night with the hair child standing over her. It should not have been able to stand, let alone haul itself onto her bed. Nor should it have been able to fist her hair in a grip so tight her scalp puckered or stuff an appendage into her mouth to block her scream. She tried to tear it apart, but the seams held. Only when she rammed it into the wall did it let go. It skittered across the room and hid somewhere that the candle she lit couldn't reach. Ogechi backed toward the door, listening, but what noise does hair make?

When the hair child jumped onto Ogechi's head she shrieked and shook herself but it gripped her hair again, tighter this time. She then did something that would follow her all her days. She raised the candle and set it on fire. And when the baby fell to the ground writhing, she covered it with a pot and held it down, long after her fingers had blistered from the heat, until the child, as tough as she'd made it, stopped moving.

Outside, she sat on the little step in front of the entrance to her apartment. No one had paid any mind to the noise—this wasn't the sort of building where one checked up on screams. Knees to her chin, Ogechi sobbed into the callused skin, feeling part relief, part something else—a sliver of empathy Mama hadn't been able to steal. There was so much dirt on the ground, so much of it everywhere, all around her. When she turned back into the room and lifted the pot, she saw all those pretty, shiny strands transformed to ash. Then she scooped the dirt into the pot and added water.

This she knew. How to make firm clay—something

she was born to do. When the mix was just right, she added a handful of the ashes. *Let this child be born in sorrow*, she told herself. *Let this child live in sorrow. Let this child not grow into a foolish, hopeful girl with joy to barter.* Ogechi formed the head, the arms, the legs. She gave it her mother's face. In the morning, she would fetch leaves to protect it from the rain.

BUCHI'S GIRLS

▲ ▼ ▲

Buchi woke to the thwack-thwack of the machete in the grass and the offended clucks of the chicken who took issue with the noise. Every few moments a ping would echo as the blade struck the stucco of the house. She counted on the sharp sound to wake her daughters. If she had her way, the girls would sleep as long as they wanted—days, months even. They had certainly earned it.

She reached a hand under Damaris, at six years old her youngest, and sighed when she felt the wetness. Precious would have her head. The little girl was supposed to sleep on the tarp-covered pallet, which crinkled with her every turn and shift, but when Damaris had sat up to watch her mother and sister snuggle into the big bed, a telltale moue on her mouth, Buchi didn't have it in her to deny her. Besides, the more bodies in the bed, the better. Sleeping alone reminded her that before she'd been mother, she'd been wife, and lover before that, and the bed needed to become something else if she was to survive.

Buchi had become an expert in interpreting her daughter's expressions, almost as good as Louisa, her eldest, who understood Damaris completely, even though the child hadn't spoken a word since her father's death. Before that, she'd been a chatty girl, inquisitive and bossy.

The blade pinged again and again. Louisa woke like a startled animal but relaxed when she saw her mother. Her smile was filmy, sadness visible underneath. It disappeared completely when she nudged her younger sister with her knee.

"Damaris wet the bed!"

"I know, baby."

"Auntie will be angry."

Buchi's throat constricted.

The thwack-thwack stopped and the runch of the rake replaced it.

"We won't tell them then. Come on, help me."

Their talking roused Damaris and the little girl

blinked awake, became aware of the damp underneath her, and started to cry.

"Shh, it's okay, honey, up, up."

Damaris raised her arms and Buchi scooped her up, then jostled and swayed her to quiet before handing her to Louisa.

In the kitchen, Buchi set a pot of water to boil and switched on the kettle. The raking had stopped and if she listened close enough she could hear Lawrence singing one of his Yoruba songs, the most sound he made other than when he spoke to the girls. His voice was terrible, but she would never risk their hard-won friendship by pointing that out, even in jest. She steeped two cups of tea and set aside a sachet of Ovaltine for the girls to share.

Lawrence approached the back door and she quickly buttered and jammed two slices of bread before the old man could object to the excess. The screen door creaked open and he stood there, waiting. Buchi didn't waste time cajoling him in. Precious had trained him too well.

"Good morning, ma."

"Good morning, Lawrence."

She handed him his cup of tea, creamy with milk and sugar, and a slice of bread. She checked the pot of water, then took her breakfast to join him on the steps. She needed this, these few quiet moments of companionship before the monotony of her day. Lawrence sipped his tea and gave little hums of satisfaction as he chewed. He was a man who enjoyed his sugar.

"Damaris wet the bed today."

He grunted, then murmured, "Sorry, oh."

Unspoken was Buchi's request that he be gentle with her daughter. Gent*ler*. When she and the girls first moved in with her sister and her husband a few months before, less than a month after Nnamdi's passing, they had been a mess. Damaris, though silent, cycled through wild mood swings. And Louisa, dear Louisa, had been so scared they would be asked to leave that she put all her effort into being so very good and so very careful, losing her impetus for play.

Lawrence, jaded no doubt by interactions with the four spoiled children of the house, who took after their mother in looks but their father in temperament, had been standoffish with the girls at first. But after the day he came across Damaris having a fit in the garden and Louisa bent over her, begging her to be quiet or "they'll send us away," he'd become softer with them. Damaris responded to the softness by

following him around, pulling weeds where he pulled
weeds and feeding the chickens, whose numbers fluc-
tuated with meals and repurchases, each fulfilling its
destiny on the plate. All save one.

Kano was a runt that one of the frequently replaced
house girls had been tricked into buying. Stuck in per-
petual adolescence, the chicken never grew or laid
eggs, and had graduated from future meal to family
pet. Buchi and Kano shared a mutual dislike for each
other, but the bird and the girls got along. Especially
Damaris, who took to the small chicken like it was her
child. They took turns following each other, and at
times the temperamental bird got something in its
head and chased Damaris around the house, and Buchi
and Louisa would laugh and laugh when she rushed
screaming past the kitchen door. Then Kano would
stop as abruptly as she'd started and peck around
Damaris's feet, and the little girl would squat by her
and play.

"Go and feed your wife," Buchi would say, handing
a chunk of bread to her daughter, and Damaris would
take it and run to the bird.

Now Kano pecked around the bottom of the
steps, awaiting their generosity. Lawrence tossed a few

crumbs her way and the pecking became frenzied. They watched the bird till Buchi heard the sizzle of boiling water hitting the burner, followed by a sound that had her gritting her teeth.

"Buchi! Buchi!" Her sister from somewhere in the house.

They all three scattered, bird, man, woman. Buchi grabbed Lawrence's half-filled cup. Precious would have a fit if she saw the man drinking out of one of her mugs. She gulped the last of her tea, choked, and was almost knocked over when Lawrence slapped her back.

"Chineke, before Madam sees you and accuses you of assault."

She was rewarded with a quiver of a smile that from reserved Lawrence might as well have been a guffaw. As soon as she had moved into her sister's house, Precious had discouraged her friendly overtures toward the servant. "You'll start giving him airs." But Buchi persisted and was repaid with his rare smiles, the care he took with her children, and a kind ear. Though he rarely offered advice, the old man was someone she could talk to. And the bits she knew about him—that he was the eldest of nine, that his mother had died only last year, that in a past life he'd been one of Abacha's drivers—were gems she'd pried from their setting.

"Buchi!" Louder now. She rushed to meet Precious before her sister sought her in the guest bedroom.

Precious held her mobile in one hand and the edges of her housecoat in the other. She didn't say anything till Buchi greeted her.

"Someone is calling for you, that your South African friend."

Buchi set the cups down and snatched the phone from Precious.

"Ijeoma, kedu?"

"It is well, how are you?" Ijeoma replied. But Buchi, aware of Precious's presence behind her, couldn't answer as honestly as she would have liked.

"We are fine, my dear. Sorry, I forgot to charge my phone."

They continued with little pleasantries, Buchi steering the conversation from dangerous territory until she could politely step away from Precious's hearing. She turned to smile at her sister and froze when she spotted Precious sipping from the half-empty cup. Lawrence's cup. She was looking at the mess of crumbs Buchi hadn't had a chance to clear, and frowning. Buchi took that moment to make her exit.

She held her snicker till she moved into the hallway where her sister's children had their rooms. They stood empty now, the children at boarding school in the UK.

"Why are you laughing?"

Buchi told Ijeoma of Precious and the mug, and the other woman laughed too.

"Good, she behaves too somehow; you know I've never liked her."

Ijeoma was her oldest friend, close since primary school, closer still in secondary. They'd been chief bridesmaids at each other's weddings and had reached most milestones together, getting married and having their first children less than a year apart. Other milestones too . . .

Ijeoma had lost her only daughter to sickle cell complications months before Buchi lost Nnamdi to the road accident. Ijeoma's rage at the country's ineptitude—they'd taken Soma to two hospitals, miles apart, before they'd found someone who could treat her—had driven her to South Africa after the death. And she was thinking of the US still.

Buchi stopped in the doorway of her nieces' room, a treasure trove of Barbies and the like, and leaned into the frame. She would have gone inside but Precious had forbidden it of her and the girls. She didn't want her daughters to return and find their room "messed up" or their toys missing.

"I hate this house. It hasn't been good for them."

Ijeoma's silence invited reconsideration.

"Well, it's been a bit good for Damaris, I guess, but it's turning Louisa into a jumpy mouse."

"Have you given any thought to my suggestion? I ran it by Onyeka and he's fine with it."

The suggestion entailed Buchi sending Louisa to live with her friend under the guise that she was Ijeoma's dead daughter. The death certificate had yet to be processed even after all this time, and probably never would be. The girls even shared an age, twelve. Louisa could simply take Soma's name, slip into her life.

"Please send her, we could always use some help around here."

My daughter needs help, not to be help, Buchi thought, but that was unfair, and the words stayed in her throat. Ijeoma had six children to Buchi's two, and the eldest girl was no longer around to ease the burden.

"We'll see," she told her friend, but she knew her answer. There were some things a mother just couldn't do.

They wound the conversation down with chit-chat of people they knew, till it puttered out and they disconnected. Buchi peeked into the kitchen. Finding the room empty, she slipped the phone into her sister's hiding spot on the counter, behind the canister of sugar. Then she grabbed the pot of water, now half boiled away, and emptied it into a bucket. In the guest room, Louisa had stripped Damaris and the younger girl was sprawled naked on the floor, writing in an old activity book, content for now.

Louisa had also stripped the bed and piled the soggy sheets in the corner. Buchi joined her older daughter and they went to work, sponging the mattress, scrubbing it with Omo, and sponging again, till the wetness was simply water that would dry to a less pungent finish. In that moment, Louisa scrubbing alongside her, Buchi was grateful for her daughter's turnabout obedient nature and knew that as much as she worried over it, she'd also come to rely on it.

Between the two of them they got the sheets clean, Damaris bathed and dressed, and all of them readied for the day. The girls' breakfast was Golden Morn and the shared Ovaltine sachet rationed from the box Precious'd bought for her kids and wouldn't replenish till they returned.

Damaris finished first and went to stand by Buchi, expectant. Buchi looked at Louisa.

"She wants to feed Kano something."

Damaris cupped her hands together, activity book clutched in the crook of her armpit, and Buchi tipped a generous helping of dry cereal into them. The chicken met her daughter at the door, their standing date, and Damaris piled the food at the bottom of the steps. Then she opened the book and began to . . . write? Draw?

"What is she doing?"

"I don't know, writing something about Kano, I think. She won't let me see."

Louisa shrugged, then gathered their bowls and cups and took them to the sink, where she washed them and the two mugs already there. Then she looked around for another way to be useful.

"No, go on outside." Louisa went and sat a step above Damaris, reading the book over her shoulder. Whatever she saw made her smile, a genuine one.

The rest of the morning was spent indoors, with Buchi giving the girls lessons. Damaris was learning how to write words, if not say them, and Louisa was learning more basic math. Buchi knew Louisa was bored and must have been falling behind, but basic math was all Buchi could do. That had been Nnamdi's territory, with his background as a professor of economics. He'd even enlisted Louisa unwittingly in balancing their budget, the budget of the hypothetical family in the problems he drew up, who were always managing an ever-dwindling sum of money that would be stretched and stretched. Then just when things were about to snap, the father, a hypothetical professor of divinity, would finally get paid some of his back salary or wrangle a loan from an uncle, and the stretching would begin anew.

When Buchi and Nnamdi learned of people stealing or cheating others of their share, Nnamdi would ask Buchi in private, "Is money everything?" The correct answer was no, money wasn't everything, and how foolish of people to define themselves by it. That high-mindedness felt foolish now that she couldn't afford to send her children to school.

Precious had promised to bring that up with her husband. She and Dickson left every morning by eight to go to the office where they worked together "with cement." That was all Buchi knew about the work that allowed them to buy a fantasy life with twice-yearly family vacations, and to send all four children to Ardingly with no trouble.

When the girls began to fidget, Buchi sent them back outside and began preparing both lunch for them and dinner for Precious and Dickson. That was the deal. Buchi could stay, but she'd have to earn it.

Precious hadn't even been able to look her in the eye when she'd laid out the terms—cook, clean, manage the house help—per Dickson, she'd added, like that would soften the blow. Buchi hadn't felt one way or the other about Dickson before that. He was loud, but lots of people were loud. But it took a certain meanness to require this of her when she was still managing her children's sorrow.

Buchi fueled her arm with her anger as she cleaved the meat for dinner. She worked for close to an hour, then stepped out of the humid room for some fresh air. On the steps she found a small bag of garden eggs and nestled inside, a smaller bag of peanuts. She smiled. Lawrence. She ground the nuts to butter and sliced a few garden eggs in two. One skittered off the counter and she bent to pick it up, the softness of her belly compressing into folds. *You're not fat*, Ijeoma would say, *just grief-fed*.

She called the girls and they came running, a race Louisa let her sister win. Louisa ate a garden egg with relish, while Damaris licked off the peanut butter and gave half of the bitter vegetable to her sister to finish. The other half she secreted in her fist. For that silly bird, no doubt.

Damaris rested her chin on the table while Louisa washed the plate and wiped down the counter, then followed her sister outside. Buchi watched them from the window till they ran out of sight, then sighed and returned to her chores. Louisa would do her fair share before the day was done, but Buchi tried to get to as many as she could and refused to let her daughter clean any of the bathrooms. She might have had to take shit from Precious and Dickson, who amused themselves ordering around the eager-to-please child, but that was as far as it would go.

When lunch was ready she called the girls in, and continued their lessons after. More words to trace for Damaris, and for Louisa, a passage from the Bible to read and summarize. While the girls worked, Buchi mopped, starting in the far hall in front of the master bedroom—which was kept locked in Precious and Dickson's absence—and working her way past their children's rooms. Pausing to take a breath, she glanced into their daughters' bedroom again. Pink carpet, white twin beds connected by shelves that held books and toys, one row dedicated to dolls alone. Buchi balanced on her haunches for a moment, then stepped inside. She smoothed the already smooth duvet on one of the beds and sneered. Who needed a duvet in this Nigerian heat? Oh, but it was so lovely. Twin stuffed polar bears continued the pink-and-white theme, and, in one corner, the enormous white dollhouse her girls had sighed over when they'd come to visit in the past. The dollhouse they'd played with that was now forbidden to them.

Why, Buchi suddenly thought, had Precious not locked these rooms, too? She said the open doors made the house feel like her children were still there, but why tempt the girls with what they could not have? Buchi reached into the dollhouse and picked up a perfectly miniature kitchen chair. How lovely. She broke off a leg, grabbed another perfect little chair, and broke off its leg too. She started grabbing pieces at random, snapping off edges and knobs. She whirled and started for the dolls that went with the house—who needed thirty-seven fucking dolls?—but stopped when she heard a gasp from the hallway.

Louisa stood there, wide-eyed.

"You broke it." Her daughter was looking at the front door of the dollhouse, now hanging lopsided. She couldn't see the inside, the wreckage of furniture, from where she stood.

"It's okay, honey, Mummy will fix it. Do you want to help?"

Louisa shook her head. Wild goats couldn't have dragged her into that room. But she stared at Buchi while she straightened the door, and after stepping aside to let her out, continued staring at the house, then the dolls.

"Do you want to play with one?"

Louisa nodded.

"You can play with one, just one, I won't tell anybody."

But Louisa shook her head and ran off, as though the thought was too much for her.

Buchi sighed and continued to mop. The broken doll furniture would not be discovered until the kids returned in two months—and she didn't want to think about what would happen then, the questions she would have to answer—but dirty floors would be noticed today.

By the time she reached the kitchen, the girls had finished their assignments and were playing outside. Louisa's summary sat on the table. Buchi took it with her to the bathroom. She sat on the toilet, accustomed now to the peace she got there since Louisa no longer dared to disturb her. Before, Louisa would constantly bug her and Nnamdi with requests for snacks, money to buy snacks, or complaints about why Damaris had gotten a bigger snack than she had, when she was the eldest. Nnamdi would say she was Buchi's little piglet and she would say that no, Louisa was Nnamdi's little piglet, and they would trade the greedy child back and forth, though never in her hearing. Buchi choked on something she couldn't name.

The death had been so stupid, avoidable and stupid. They'd been driving to the Enugu airport to pick up a friend, Damaris singing in the backseat, Louisa at school. They were early enough that when they saw a couple on the other side of the road flagging down help for their stalled vehicle, Nnamdi pulled over.

"Hian! See this one," Buchi said of the woman, who wore a dress so tight it sliced the pudge of her belly in two.

WHAT IT MEANS WHEN A MAN FALLS FROM THE SKY

"Be nice," Nnamdi said, smugly imitating her warning to the children when they weren't.

He closed the door and walked a little ways ahead. The sausage-casing woman started across the road, no doubt intending to cross after an oncoming lorry had passed, but the driver panicked and swerved away from her, plowing into Nnamdi so hard Buchi wouldn't have been able to identify him if she hadn't seen it. If Damaris hadn't seen it.

A knock startled her. She wiped the wet from her face and struggled to keep the tears out of her voice.

"Who is it?"

"Louisa."

"What is it, honey?"

"Can I have another garden egg?"

"You want another one?"

"Yes, is it okay?"

Is it okay? Buchi had to resist telling her she could have the whole bag, that Mummy would plant her a whole field of garden eggs, and a field of dolls, too.

"Of course you can."

And as her daughter ran, then returned to shout "Thank you" through the door, and ran to the kitchen again, Buchi found herself struggling to hold back a different set of tears.

———

When Buchi returned to the kitchen, her sister's husband was there. Dickson sat in that sprawled way of his, unself-conscious, completely believing in his right to take up space. Nnamdi had always disliked his gidi-gidi personality, said only small-minded men acted so big, and efforts to engender friendship between the two men always failed. Precious's husband was the sort of man people pretended to like because they couldn't afford not to. His presence in the kitchen disrupted the easy feel of the room. Louisa had squeezed into the corner, as far from Dickson's energy as she could get without leaving.

"Oya now, your sister said you wanted to talk to me."

That had been almost two weeks ago, but Buchi knew not to point it out.

"Yes. Louisa, you can go."

"She should stay. Is this not about her?"

Louisa looked from her uncle to her mother and Buchi put an extra warning in her eye. Louisa should leave. But it had been too long since she'd had to be so firm, and Dickson's order superseded hers. The girl stayed. Buchi sighed.

"It's about school. The girls' school fees. I, I need help with them."

Dickson sipped his water.

"Why?"

"I can't afford the proper school."

"Why not?"

He wasn't going to make it easy.

Before she formed a response that would preserve her dignity in front of her daughter, Damaris went tearing past the kitchen door screaming in her harmless way, the chicken right behind.

Dickson sucked his teeth.

"I should kill that chicken."

"No!"

This from Louisa, no longer in the corner, but close now, like she was ready to physically restrain her uncle.

"I will kill it and I will eat it with stew."

"No, you can't."

Dickson was clearly joking, a mean joke made meaner by not backing down at a child's distress, but still, a joke. But Louisa, whose world had become black and white, couldn't see that.

"You can't kill the bird, Damaris is writing a book about it."

"Book, nko? Well, she can make it a cookbook," Dickson said, and roared at his jest.

Louisa lost it then and ran up to him and beat her small fists about his head. Dickson and Buchi shared a still, shocked moment, then Buchi grabbed the girl before her uncle could return the blows.

"In my own house! A child will hit me in my own house!"

"Dickson, please," Buchi said, putting herself between him and her daughter.

"We will eat that bird tonight. We will. Lawrence!"

"You can't, you can't." Louisa was sobbing now. "Mummy, you have to stop him."

Buchi thought about the very expensive dollhouse with the very expensive broken furniture.

"Shh, Louisa, be quiet."

The look her daughter gave her was acid. Louisa ran out, and Buchi knew something had changed between them. There was only so much a mother could ask a daughter to bear before that bond became bondage.

Lawrence opened the screen door.

"Evening, sah."

"Go and kill that chicken."

Lawrence hesitated.

"Which one, sah?"

"Shut up and go, you know which one."

Buchi stepped forward to interject and was met with a quick, hot slap followed by Dickson's finger in her face.

"Not one word from you. You bring your children into my house to insult me? Me, who has let you stay here all this time? No, not one word."

Buchi always imagined herself a quiet woman whose well ran deep. That when faced with extreme conditions, she would meet them with an inner fount of strength, a will long dormant electrified to life. But these last few months of folding into herself, of enduring one petty disgrace after another, had drained that well dry.

As the insult throbbed in her cheek, she did not retaliate, did not raise her hand and slap him back. She was never more aware that nothing, not even the food that nourished her children's bodies, not even her dignity, belonged to her. Dickson lowered his arm. This was a point he would never have to make again.

He left the kitchen and Buchi trembled in his wake. She went outside to find Lawrence holding his machete and looking at Kano, who pecked at his leather sandals like she could taste the salt of sweat. Lawrence looked at Buchi, then back at the bird.

"Damaris?" she asked.

"In the veranda, ma. With her book."

They shared a moment in quiet thought.

"I won't do it, oh. There are other chickens, why must it be this one?"

"Lawrence, please, just do it."

"I won't, it isn't—"

"Just kill the bloody bird or I'll do it myself!"

She was crying now and didn't know how to stop.

Lawrence took hold of her elbow to guide her to sit, and Buchi exploded.

"Get your hands off me. Who do you think you are, get your hands off me."

The old man's eyes shuttered. He removed his hand from her elbow and walked away. Kano followed him, clucking her disagreement with his speed.

Buchi walked around the house, toward the veranda, thinking of irreparable damage, thinking of women bled dry, thinking of Damaris, thinking of Louisa, dear, brave Louisa, who deserved something she could not give. And Buchi knew she would pick up the phone, call Ijeoma, and do something a mother just couldn't do.

Dinner was quiet. Damaris speared her bit of beef
and chewed all the juice out of it before spitting the
fibrous ligaments onto her plate. She didn't seem to
notice the tension around the kitchen table or how
extra nice Buchi was to Louisa, or how Louisa took
sullen little bites of rice and all but ignored her mother.
In the dining room, Dickson and Precious talked,
though Precious, who usually acknowledged Buchi
with a thank-you or complimented the meal, ignored
her, too. Buchi dreaded the lecture she knew was coming, about how a wife must stand with her husband
and how she, Buchi, should not let the devil use her to
bring strife into Precious's marriage. Dickson raised a
brow and gave Precious a look but made no comment
about the lack of chicken on his plate. Buchi would be
hearing about that, too.

Lawrence, who usually handed her the freshly
slaughtered chickens, had put Kano in a bucket on the
back steps and covered it, in case Damaris walked by.
And she did, looking for the bird, but was placated
with the news that Kano had gone "outside," meaning
outside the gate, something the bird did often despite

Precious's complaints that it made them look like bush people. The bird hadn't been drained properly. Blood pooled into her feathers, and the ragged seam at her neck signaled Lawrence's distaste for the task. Devoid of life, Kano's body shrank. Picked clean off the bone, her flesh wouldn't amount to a man's fist. Buchi bagged the bird and threw her onto the trash heap outside that, when Lawrence lit it, would become her funeral pyre.

After dinner, Louisa took Damaris to bathe while Buchi washed the dishes and cleaned the kitchen. When she'd completed her tasks, she went out onto the back steps and waited for Lawrence, who usually sat with her for a few minutes, both of them exhausted from a day filled with work that needed four bodies, not two. He soon approached the steps and, fearing that he wouldn't stop, Buchi called out to him.

"Good night, ma," he said, but he kept walking toward his quarters, a small cement structure built into the walls that surrounded the house. Buchi sighed and shook her head. Enough tears today.

Louisa had already put Damaris to bed on her pallet and the little girl was gone from this world. Buchi sat on her own bed and patted the spot next to her. Louisa hesitated, but got up and sat next to her mother. Buchi tried to rub circles into her daughter's back, but Louisa shrugged her off.

"Are you all right?"

Louisa didn't respond, which meant a no she was too polite to voice.

Buchi pressed on.

"Do you know why I had to listen to Uncle Dickson?"

Because we are destitute.

Because your father was a fool and, yes, money is everything.

Because the consequences of disrespecting a man like Dickson are always disproportionate to the sin. A grenade in retaliation for a slap. A world undone for a girl's mistake.

Louisa shrugged.

"Do you remember Auntie Ijeoma?" Buchi asked.

Louisa nodded.

"Do you want to visit her?"

Another nonresponse.

"Please, Louisa, I can't have you not talking as well. Please."

Louisa finally looked at her.

"Soma," she said.

The two girls had only met a few times, as distance and time constraints meant that Buchi and Ijeoma didn't get together as much as they wanted, but Louisa had been at the funeral, knew that the girl was gone. Soma, indeed. So quiet in that way a girl in a family of boys could be. Buchi had often told Nnamdi she wished they lived closer so that Soma could be a tempering influence on Louisa, to which Nnamdi had responded that Louisa was too like her mother. *You might as well bite into a diamond.*

A light knock preceded Precious's opening the door—the door that Buchi was never to lock. She nodded in her sister's direction before walking off. Buchi was being summoned. She looked at Damaris, splayed and boneless in sleep, and knew that the little girl's problems were ones she could resolve: tears she could wipe, mattresses she could scrub, a distressed body she could clutch close to her as it kicked and screamed. Locks with keys she held.

"You like Auntie Ijeoma, don't you?"

But the question was just a formality at this point.

WHAT IT MEANS WHEN A MAN
FALLS FROM THE SKY

▲ ▼ ▲

t means twenty-four-hour news coverage. It means
politicians doing damage control, activists egging on
protests. It means Francisco Furcal's granddaughter at
a press conference defending her family's legacy.

"My grandfather's formula is sound. Math is constant and absolute. Any problems that arise are the
fault of those who miscalculate it."

Bad move, lady. This could only put everyone on the
defensive, compelling them to trot out their transcripts
and test results and every other thing that proved their
genius. Nneoma tried to think of where she'd put her
own documents after the move, but that led to thinking

of where she'd moved from, which led to thinking of whom she'd left behind.

Best not to venture there. Best instead to concentrate on the shaky footage captured by a security camera. The motion-activated device had caught the last fifty feet of the man's fall, the windmill panic of flailing arms, the spread of his body on the ground. When the formula for flight had been revealed short months before, the ceremony had started unimpressively enough, with a man levitating like a monk for fifteen boring minutes before shooting into the air. The scientific community was agog. What did it mean that the human body could now defy things humanity had never thought to question, like gravity? It had seemed like the start of a new era.

Now the newscast jumped to the Mathematicians who'd discovered the equation for flight. They were being ambushed by gleeful reporters at parties, while picking up their children in their sleek black cars, on their vacations, giving a glimpse of luxury that was foreign to the majority of the viewing public, who must have enjoyed the embarrassed faces and defensive outbursts from well-fed mouths.

By blaming the Mathematicians instead of the Formula, Martina Furcal and the Center created a maelstrom around the supposedly infallible scientists while protecting her family's legacy. And their money. Maybe not such a bad move after all.

Nneoma flipped through the channels, listening closely. If the rumor that Furcal's Formula was beginning to unravel around the edges gained any traction, it would eventually trickle down to the twenty-four hundred Mathematicians like her, who worked around the globe, making their living calculating and subtracting emotions, drawing them from living bodies like poison from a wound.

She was one of the fifty-seven registered Mathematicians who specialized in calculating grief, down from the fifty-nine of last year. Alvin Claspell, the Australian, had committed suicide after, if the stories were to be believed, going mad and trying to eat himself. This work wasn't for everyone. And of course Kioni Mutahi had simply disappeared, leaving New Kenya with only one grief worker.

There were six grief workers in the Biafra-Britannia Alliance, where Nneoma now lived, the largest concentration of grief workers in any province to serve the largest concentration of the grieving. Well, the largest concentration that could pay.

It was the same footage over and over. Nneoma

offed the unit. The brouhaha would last only as long as it took the flight guys to wise up and blame the fallen man for miscalculating. "Cover your ass," as the North American saying went, though there wasn't much of that continent left to speak it.

A message dinged on the phone console and Nneoma hurried to press it, eager, then embarrassed at her eagerness, then further embarrassed when it wasn't even Kioni, just her assistant reminding her of the lecture she was to give at the school. She deleted the message—of course she remembered—and became annoyed. She thought, again, of getting rid of the young woman. But sometimes you need an assistant, such as when your girlfriend ends your relationship with the same polite coolness that she initiated it, leaving you to pack and relocate three years' worth of shit in one week. Assistants come in handy then. But that was eight weeks ago and Nneoma was over it. Really, she was.

She gathered her papers and rang for the car, which pulled up to the glass doors almost immediately. Amadi was timely like that. Her mother used to say that she could call him on her way down the stairs and open the door to find him waiting. Mama was gone now, and Nneoma's father, who'd become undone, never left the house. Amadi had run his errands for him until Nneoma moved back from New Kenya, when her father gifted him to her, like a basket of fine cheese. She'd accepted the driver as what she knew he was, a peace offering. And though it would never be the same between them, she called her father every other Sunday.

She directed Amadi to go to the store first. They drove through the wide streets of Enugu and passed a playground full of sweaty egg-white children. It wasn't that Nneoma had a problem with the Britons per se, but some of her father had rubbed off on her. At his harshest Papa would call them refugees rather than allies. He'd long been unwelcome in polite company.

"They come here with no country of their own and try to take over everything and don't contribute anything," he often said.

That wasn't entirely true.

When the floods started swallowing the British Isles, they'd reached out to Biafra, a plea for help that was answered. Terms were drawn, equitable exchanges of services contracted. But while one hand reached out for help, the other wielded a knife. Once here, the Britons had insisted on having their own lands and their own separate government. A compromise, aided by

the British threat to deploy biological weapons, re-
sulted in the Biafra-Britannia Alliance. Shared lands,
shared government, shared grievances. Her father was
only a boy when it happened but still held bitterly
to the idea of Biafran independence, an independence
his parents had died for in the late 2030s. He wasn't
alone, but most people knew to keep their opinions
to themselves, especially if their daughter was a Mathematician, a profession that came with its own set
of troubles. And better a mutually beneficial, if un-
wanted, alliance than what the French had done in
Senegal, the Americans in Mexico.

As Amadi drove, he kept the rearview mirror partially trained on her, looking for an opening to start a
chat that would no doubt lead to his suggesting they
swing by her father's place later, just for a moment, just
to say hello. Nneoma avoided eye contact. She couldn't
see her father, not for a quick hello, not today, not ever.

They pulled up to ShopRite and Nneoma hopped
out. Her stomach grumbling, she loaded more fruit in
her basket than she could eat in a week and cut the
bread queue, to the chagrin of the waiting customers.
The man at the counter recognized her and handed
over the usual selection of rolls and the crusty ba-
guette she would eat with a twinge of guilt. The

French didn't get money directly, yet she couldn't stop feeling like she was funding the idea of them. Ignoring the people staring at her, wondering who she might be (a diplomat? a minister's girlfriend?), she walked the edges of the store, looping toward the checkout lane.

Then she felt him.

Nneoma slowed and picked up a small box of detergent, feigning interest in the instructions to track him from the corner of her eye. He was well dressed, but not overly so. He looked at her, confused, not sure why he was so drawn to her. Nneoma could feel the sadness rolling off him and she knew if she focused she'd be able to see his grief, clear as a splinter. She would see the source of it, its architecture, and the way it anchored to him. And she would be able to remove it.

It started when she was fourteen, in math class. She'd always been good at math but had no designs on being a Mathematician. No one did. It wasn't a profession you chose or aspired to; either you could do it or you couldn't. That day, the teacher had shown them a long string of Furcal's Formula, purchased from the Center like a strain of virus. To most of the other students, it was an impenetrable series of numbers and symbols, but to Nneoma it was as simple as the alphabet. Seeing the Formula unlocked something in her. From then on she could see a person's sadness as plainly as the clothes he wore.

The Center paid for the rest of her schooling, paid off the little debt her family owed, and bought them a new house. They trained her to hone her talents, to go beyond merely seeing a person's grief to mastering how to remove it. She'd been doing it for so long she could exorcise the deepest of traumas for even the most re-sistant of patients. Then her mother died.

The man in the store stood there looking at her and Nneoma took advantage of his confusion to walk away. The grieving were often drawn to her, an inadvertent magnetic thing. It made her sheltered life blessed and necessary. The Center was very understanding and helped contracted Mathematicians screen their clients. None of them were ever forced to work with a client or provide a service they didn't want to. Nneoma worked almost exclusively with parents who'd lost a child, wealthy couples who'd thought death couldn't touch them, till it did. When the Center partnered with gov-ernments to work with their distressed populations, the job was voluntary and most Mathematicians do-nated a few hours a week. There were exceptions, like

Kioni, who worked with such people full-time, and Nneoma, who didn't work with them at all. Mother Kioni, Nneoma had called her, first with affection, then with increasing malice as things between them turned ugly. This man, in the tidy suit and good shoes, was more along the lines of her preferred clientele. He could very well become a client of hers in the future, but not today, not like this.

At checkout, the boy who scanned and bagged her groceries was wearing a name tag that read "Martin," which may or may not have been his name. The Britons preferred their service workers with names they could pronounce, and most companies obliged them. The tattoo on his wrist indicated his citizenship—an original Biafran—and his class, third. No doubt he lived outside of the city and was tracked from the minute he crossed the electronic threshold till the minute he finished his shift and left. He was luckier than most.

At the car, she checked her personal phone, the number only her father, her assistant, and Kioni knew. Still no message. She hadn't heard from Kioni since she'd moved out. She had to know Nneoma worried, in spite of how they'd left things. None of their mutual New Kenyan contacts knew where to find her, and

Kioni's phone went unanswered. Maybe this was what it took for Kioni to exorcise her.

On the way to the school, Nneoma finished off two apples and a roll and flipped through her notes. She had done many such presentations, which were less about presenting and more about identifying potential Mathematicians, who had a way of feeling each other out. She ran a finger along the Formula, still mesmerized by it after all this time. She'd brought fifty-seven lines of it, though she would only need a few to test the students.

When things began to fall apart, the world cracked open by earthquakes and long-dormant volcanoes stretched, yawned, and bellowed, the churches (mosques, temples) fell—not just the physical buildings shaken to dust by tremors, but the institutions as well. Into the vacuum stepped Francisco Furcal, a Chilean mathematician who discovered a formula that explained the universe. It, like the universe, was infinite, and the idea that the formula had no end and, perhaps, by extension, humanity had no end was exactly what the world needed.

Over decades, people began to experiment with this infinite formula and, in the process, discovered equations that coincided with the anatomy of the human body, making work like hers possible. A computer at the Center ran the Formula 24/7, testing its infiniteness. There were thousands and thousands of lines. People used to be able to tour the South African branch and watch the endless symbols race ticker-style across a screen. Then the Center closed to the public, and the rumors started that Furcal's Formula was wrong, that the logic of it faltered millions and millions of permutations down the line, past anything a human could calculate in her lifetime. That it was not infinite.

They were just that, rumors, but then a man fell from the sky.

As they neared the school, they could see a few protesters with gleaming electronic placards. The angry red of angry men. Amadi slowed.

"Madam?"

"Keep going, there are only ten."

But the number could triple by the time she was ready to leave. How did they always know where she'd be?

The car was waved through the school's outer gate, then the inner gate, where Amadi's ID was checked, then double-checked. When the guard decided that Amadi wasn't credentialed enough to wait within the inner gate, Nneoma stepped in. Her driver, her rules. The guard conceded as she'd known he would, and Amadi parked the car under a covered spot out of the sun. Nneoma was greeted by Nkem Ozechi, the headmaster, a small, neat woman whose hands reminded her of Kioni's. She had a smug air about her and walked with a gait that was entirely too pleased with itself. She spoke to Nneoma as though they'd known each other for years. On a different day, Nneoma might have been charmed, interested, but today she just wanted the session to be over with so she could go home.

The class was filled with bored faces, most around thirteen or fourteen (had she ever looked so young?), few caring or understanding what she did, too untouched by tragedy to understand her necessity. But schools like these, which gathered the best and brightest that several nations had to offer (according to Nkem Ozechi), paid the Center handsomely to have people like her speak, and it was the easiest money she earned.

"How many of you can look at someone and know that they are sad?"

The whole class raised their hands.

"How many of you can tell if someone is sad even if they are not crying?"

Most hands stayed up.

"How many of you can look at a person who is sad, know why they are sad, and fix it?"

All hands lowered. She had their attention now.

The talk lasted fifteen minutes before she brought it to a close.

"Some Mathematicians remove pain, some of us deal in negative emotions, but we all fix the equation of a person. The bravest"—she winked—"have tried their head at using the Formula to make the human body defy gravity, for physical endeavors like flight."

The class giggled, the fallen man fresh in their minds.

"Furcal's Formula means that one day the smartest people can access the very fabric of the universe." For many the Formula was God, misunderstood for so long. They believed that it was only a matter of time before someone discovered the formula to create life, rather than to just manipulate it. But this was beyond the concerns of the teenagers, who applauded politely.

The headmaster stepped from the corner to moderate questions. The first were predictable and stupid. "Can you make people fall in love?" No. "Can you make someone become invisible?" No. Nkem Ozechi might have been embarrassed to know that their questions were no different from those posed by students in the lower schools. Then (again predictably) someone posed a nonquestion.

"What you are doing is wrong." From a reed-thin boy with large teeth. Despite his thinness there was a softness to him, a pampered look.

Nneoma put her hand up to stop Nkem Ozechi from interrupting. She could handle this. "Explain."

"Well, my dad says what you people do is wrong, that you shouldn't be stopping a person from feeling natural hardships. That's what it means to be human."

Someone in the back started to clap until Nneoma again raised her hand for silence. She studied the boy. He was close enough for her to note his father's occupation on his wrist (lawyer) and his class (first). She'd argued down many a person like his father, people who'd lived easy lives, who'd had moderate but manageable difficulties, then dared to compare their meager hardship with unfathomable woes.

"Your father and those people protesting outside have no concept of what real pain is. As far as I'm concerned, their feelings on this matter are invalid. I would never ask a person who hasn't tasted a dish whether it needs more salt."

The boy sat with his arms crossed, pouting. She hadn't changed his mind, you never could with people like that, but she'd shut him up.

In the quiet that followed, another hand raised. *Not her*, Nneoma thought, *not her*. She'd successfully ignored the girl since walking into the classroom. She didn't need to look at her wrist to know that the girl was Senegalese and had been affected by the Elimination. It was etched all over her, this sorrow.

"So you can make it go away?" They could have been the only two people in the room.

"Yes, I can." And to kill her dawning hope, "But it is a highly regulated and very expensive process. Most of my clients are heavily subsidized by their governments, but even then"—in case any hope remained—"you have to be a citizen."

The girl lowered her eyes to her lap, fighting tears. As though to mock her, she was flanked by a map on the wall, the entire globe splayed out as it had been seventy years ago and as it was now. Most of what had been North America was covered in water and a sea had replaced Europe. Russia was a soaked grave. The only continents unclaimed in whole or in part by the sea were Australia and the United Countries—what had once been Africa. The Elimination began after a moment of relative peace, after the French had won the trust of their hosts. The Senegalese newspapers that issued warnings were dismissed as conspiracy rags, rabble-rousers inventing trouble. But then came the camps, the raids, and the mysterious illness that wiped out millions. Then the cabinet members murdered in their beds. And the girl had survived it. To be here, at a school like this, on one of the rare scholarships offered to displaced children, the girl must have lived through the unthinkable. The weight of her mourning was too much. Nneoma left the room, followed by Nkem Ozechi, who clicked hurriedly behind her.

"Maybe some of them will be Mathematicians, like you."

Nneoma needed to gather herself. She saw the sign for the ladies' room and stepped inside, swinging the door in Nkem Ozechi's face. None of those children would ever be Mathematicians; the room was as bare of genius as a pool of fish.

She checked the stalls to make sure she was alone and bent forward to take deep breaths. She rarely worked with refugees, *true* refugees, for this reason. The complexity of their suffering always took something from her. The only time she'd felt anything as strongly was after her mother had passed and her father was in full lament, listing to the side of ruin. How could Nneoma tell him that she couldn't even look at him without being broken by it? He would never understand. The day she'd tried to work on him, to eat her father's grief, she finally understood why it was forbidden to work on close family members. Their grief was your own and you could never get out of your head long enough to calculate it. The attempt had ended with them both sobbing, holding each other in comfort and worry, till her father became so angry at the futility of it, the uselessness of her talents in this one crucial moment, that he'd said words he could not take back.

The bathroom door creaked open. Nneoma knew who it was. The girl couldn't help but seek her out. They stared at each other awhile, the girl uncertain, till Nneoma held out her arms and the girl walked into them. Nneoma saw the sadness in her eyes and began to plot the results of it on an axis. At one point the girl's mother shredded by gunfire. Her brother taken in the night by a gang of thugs. Her father falling to the synthesized virus that attacked all the melanin in his skin till his body was an open sore. And other, smaller hurts: Hunger so deep she'd swallowed fistfuls of mud. Hiding from the men who'd turned on her after her father died. Sneaking into her old neighborhood to see new houses filled with the more fortunate of the French evacuees, those who hadn't been left behind to drown, their children chasing her away with rocks like she was a dog. Nneoma looked at every last suffering, traced the edges, weighed the mass. And then she took it.

No one had ever really been able to explain what happened then, why one person could take another person's grief. Mathematical theories abounded based on how humans were, in the plainest sense, a bulk of atoms held together by positives and negatives, a type of cellular math. An equation all their own. A theologian might have called it a miracle, a kiss of grace from God's own mouth. Philosophers opined that it was actually the patients who gave up their sadness. But in that room it simply meant that a girl had an unbearable burden and then she did not.

The ride home was silent. Amadi, sensing her disquiet, resisted the casual detour he usually made past

the junction that led to her father's house, whenever
they ventured to this side of town. At home, Nneoma
went straight to bed, taking two of the pills that would
let her sleep for twelve hours. After that she would be
as close to normal as she could be. The rawness of
the girl's memories would diminish, becoming more
like a story in a book she'd once read. The girl would
feel the same way. Sleep came, deep and black, a
dreamless thing with no light.

The next morning, she turned on the unit to see
much the same coverage as the day before, except
now the fallen man's widow had jumped into the
fray, calling for a full audit of the Center's records
and of Furcal's Formula. Nneoma snorted. It was
the sort of demand that would win public support, but
the truth was the only experts who knew enough
to audit anything all worked for the Center, and it
would take them decades to pore over every line of
the formula. More likely this was a ploy for a payoff, which the woman would get. The Furcals could
afford it.

Nneoma told herself she wouldn't check her messages again for at least another hour and prepared for
her daily run. A quick peek revealed that no messages

were waiting anyway. She keyed the code into the gate to lock it behind her, stretched, and launched.

The run cleared the last vestiges of yesterday's ghosts. She would call Claudine today to see how serious this whole falling thing was. There'd be only so much the PR rep could legally say, but dinner and a few drinks might loosen her tongue. Nneoma lengthened her stride the last mile home, taking care to ease into it. The last time she'd burst into a sprint she pulled a muscle, and the pain eater assigned to her was a grim man with a nonexistent bedside manner. She'd felt his disapproval as he worked on her. No doubt he thought his talents wasted in her cozy sector and was tolerating this rotation till he could get back to the camps. Nneoma disliked Mathematicians like him and they disliked ones like her. It was a miracle she and Kioni had lasted as long as they did.

As she cleared the corner around her compound, she saw a small crowd gathered at her gate. *Protesters?* she wondered in shock before she registered the familiar faces of her neighbors. When she neared, a man she recognized but could not name caught her by the shoulders.

"We called medical right away. She was banging on

your gate and screaming. She is your friend, no? I've seen her with you before." He looked very concerned, and suddenly Nneoma didn't want to know who was there to see her and why.

It was just a beggar. The woman wore no shoes and her toes were wounds. How on earth had she been able to bypass city security? Nneoma scrambled back when the woman reached out for her, but froze when she saw her fingers, delicate and spindly, like insect legs.

Those hands had once stroked her body. She had once kissed those palms and drawn those fingers into her mouth. She would have recognized them any-where.

"Kioni?"

"Nneoma, we have to go, we have to go now." Kioni was frantic and kept looking behind her. Every bare inch of her skin was scratched or bitten or cut in some way. Her usually neat coif of dreadlocks was half miss-ing, her scalp raw and puckered as if someone had yanked them out. The smell that rolled from her was all sewage.

"Oh my God, Kioni, oh my God."

Kioni grabbed her wrists and wouldn't surrender them. "We have to go!"

Nneoma tried to talk around the horrified pit in her stomach. "Who did this to you? Where do we have to go?"

Kioni shook her head and sank to her knees. Nneoma tried to free one of her hands and when she couldn't, pressed and held the metal insert under her palm that would alert security at the Center. They would know what to do.

From her current angle, Nneoma could see more of the damage on the other woman, the scratches and bites concentrated below the elbow. Something nagged and nagged at her. And then she remembered the Australian, and the stories of him trying to eat himself.

"Kioni, who did this?" Nneoma repeated, though her suspicion was beginning to clot into certainty and she feared the answer.

Kioni continued shaking her head and pressed her lips together like a child refusing to confess a lie.

Their falling-out had started when Nneoma did the unthinkable. In violation of every boundary of their relationship (and a handful of Center rules), she'd asked Kioni to work on her father. Kioni, who volunteered herself to the displaced Senegalese and Algerians and Burkinababes and even the evacuees, anyone in dire need of a grief worker, was the last person she should have asked for such a thing, and told her so. Nneoma had called her sanctimonious, and Kioni had called her a spoiled rich girl who thought her pain was more important than it actually was. And then Kioni had asked her to leave.

Now she needed to get Kioni to the Center. Whatever was happening had to be fixed.

"They just come and they come and they come."

Nneoma crouched down to hear Kioni better. Most of her neighbors had moved beyond hearing distance, chased away by the smell. "Who comes?" she asked, trying to keep Kioni with her.

"All of them, can't you see?"

She began to understand what was happening to her former girlfriend.

How many people had Kioni worked with over the last decade? Five thousand? Ten? Ten thousand traumas in her psyche, squeezing past each other, vying for the attention of their host. What would happen if you couldn't forget, if every emotion from every person whose grief you'd eaten came back up? It could happen, if something went wrong with the formula millions and millions of permutations down the line. A thousand falling men landing on you.

Nneoma tried to retreat, to close her eyes and

unsee, but she couldn't. Instinct took over and she raced to calculate it all. The breadth of it was so vast. Too vast.

The last clear thought she would ever have was of her father, how crimson his burden had been when she'd tried to shoulder it, and how very pale it all seemed now.

GLORY

▲ ▼ ▲

When Glory's parents christened her Glorybeto-god Ngozi Akunyili, they did not foresee Facebook's "real name" policy, nor the weeks she would spend populating forms and submitting copies of her bills and driver's license and the certificate that documented her birth on September 9, 1986, a rainy Tuesday, at 6:45 p.m., after six hours of labor and six years of barrenness. Pinning on her every hope they had yet to realize, her parents imagined the type of life well-situated Igbos imagined for their children. She would be a smart girl with the best schooling. She would attend church regularly and never stray from the Word. (Amen!) She would learn to cook like her grandmother, her father added, to which her mother countered, why not like her mother, and Glorybeto-god's father hemmed and hawed till his wife said maybe he should go and eat at his mother's house. But back to Glorybetogod, whom everyone called Glory except for her grandfather, who called her "that girl" the first time he saw her.

"That girl has something rotten in her, her chi is not well."

Husband pulled wife out of the room to prevent a brawl ("I don't care how old that drunk is, I will fix his mouth today") and begged his father to accept his firstborn grandchild. He didn't see, as the grandfather did, the caul of misfortune covering Glory's face that would affect every decision she made, causing her to err on the side of wrong, time and time again. When Glory was five she decided, after much consideration, to stick her finger into the maw of a sleeping dog. At seven, shortly after her family relocated to the US, Glory thought it a good idea to walk home when her mother was five minutes late picking her up from school, a choice that saw her lost and sobbing in a Piggly Wiggly parking lot before night fell. She did a lot of things out of spite, the source of which she couldn't identify—as if she'd been born resenting the world.

That's how, much to her parents' embarrassment, their Glory came to be nearing thirty, chronically single, and working at a call center in downtown Minneapolis. She fielded calls from disgruntled homeowners on the brink of foreclosure, reading from a script that was intricate and logical and written by people who had never before spoken on the phone to a human being. In all their calculations about her future, Glory's parents had never imagined that on April 16, 2013, after receiving yet another e-mail denying her request to restore her Facebook page (the rep refused to believe any parent would actually name their child Glorybetogod), their daughter would be the sort of person for whom this flake of misfortune set rolling an avalanche of misery that quickly led to her contemplating taking her own life.

She called her mother, hoping to be talked out of it, but got her voice mail and then a text saying, What is it now? (Glory knew better than to respond.) A call to her father would yield an even cooler response, and so she spent the evening on the edge of her bed, neck tense as a fist, contemplating how a bottle of Moscato would pair with thirty gelcap sleeping pills. The note she wrote read, *I was born under an unlucky star and my destiny has caught up with me. I'm sorry, Mummy and Daddy, that I didn't complete law school and become the person you'd hoped. But it was also your fault for putting so much pressure on me. Good-bye.*

All of this was true, and not. Her parents did put pressure on her, but it was the sort of hopeful pressure that might have encouraged a better person. And she was unlucky, yes, but it was less fate and more her propensity for arguing with professors and storming out of classrooms never to return that saw her almost flunk out of college. She eventually graduated, with an embarrassing GPA. Then came law school, to which she gained entrance through a favor of a friend of a friend of her father's, thinking that her argumentative tendencies could be put to good use. But she'd managed to screw that up, too, choosing naps instead of class and happy hours instead of studying, unable to do right no matter how small the choice. These foolish little choices incremented into probation, then a polite request to leave, followed by an impolite request to leave after she'd staged a protest in the dean's office.

Glory fell asleep after a glass and a half of wine and woke to find the pills a melted mass in her fist. In the morning light, her melodramatic note embarrassed her and she tore it up and flushed it down the toilet. At work, avoiding the glare of her supervisor and the finger he pointed at the clock, she switched on her headphones to receive the first call: Mrs. Dumfries. Her husband had died and she had no clue where any paperwork was. Could Glory help her keep her house? Glory read from her script, avoiding the *no* they were never allowed to utter. Then Glen, who was actually Greg, who was also Peter, who called every day at least four or five times and tried to trick the customer service reps into promises they couldn't keep. Little did he know that even if Glory promised him his childhood home complete with all the antiques that had gone missing after the foreclosure, she would only be fired and he would still be stuck in the same two-bedroom apartment with his kids. All day the calls came in and Glory had to say no without saying *no* and the linguistic acrobatics required to evade this simple answer wore away her nerves.

At lunch, she ate one of the burritos that came three-for-a-dollar at the discount grocery store and a nice-looking sandwich that belonged to one of her coworkers, and checked her e-mail again. Then she walked by the lobby of the advertising agency that dominated the top two floors of the building. To the right of the glass lobby doors were mounted the logos of the companies the firm had branded. She paused and took a photo of herself in front of the logo of the jewelry megachain. If her Facebook page was ever restored, she would post the picture, with the caption "Worked on my favorite account today. The best part is the free samples!"

Then her cousin in Port Harcourt would like her post, and another friend would confess her envy, and others still would say how (OMG!) she was *sooo* lucky. And for a moment she would live the sort of life her parents had imagined for her those many, many years ago.

After her lunch break, she sank back into her seat and was about to switch her headset on when he walked in. Glory knew he was Nigerian right away by his gait. And when he spoke, a friendly greeting as he shook her supervisor's hand, her guess was confirmed. He wore a suit, slightly ill fitting, but his shoulders made up for it. He joined a group of trainees across the room.

He had an air of competence she found irritating, reading from the script as though he had it memorized, managing to make it sound compassionate and genuine. At one point he noticed her staring, and

every time she looked at him after that he was looking
at her, too.

She culled bits and pieces of him over the rest of
the day, eavesdropped from impressed supervisors
who sang his praises. He was getting an MBA at the U.
He'd grown up in Nigeria but visited his uncle in At-
lanta every summer. After his MBA he was going to
attend law school. His parents were both doctors.

Glory knew what he was doing, because she did the
same: sharing too many details of her life with these
strangers, signaling why she didn't belong here earning
$13.50 an hour. She was better than "customer service
representative"—everyone should know that this title
was only temporary. Except in his case, it was all true.

He smiled at her when she was leaving, a smile so
sure of reciprocation that Glory wanted to flip him
off. But the home training that lingered caused her to
avert her eyes instead and hurry to catch the bus.

Her phone dinged. A text from her mother. Why did
you call me, do you need money again? *No*, she wanted to
respond, *I'm doing fine*, but she didn't. After a week,
her mother might send $500 and say this was the last
time and she'd better not tell her father. Glory would
use the money to complete her rent or buy new shoes

WHAT IT MEANS WHEN A MAN FALLS FROM THE SKY

or maybe squirrel it away to be nibbled bit by bit—
candy here, takeout there—till it disappeared. Then,
when her mother couldn't restrain herself anymore,
Glory would receive a stern, long-winded lecture via
e-mail, about how she wouldn't have to worry about
such things if she were married, and why didn't she let
her father introduce her to some of the young men at
his work? And Glory would delete it, and cry, and
retrace all the missteps that had led her to this par-
ticular place. She knew her birth story and what her
grandfather had said, but it never made a difference
when the time came to make the right choice. She was
always drawn to the wrong one, like a dog curious to
taste its own vomit.

The next day, Glory arrived at work to see the man
sitting in the empty spot next to hers.

"Good morning."

"Hi."

"My name is Thomas. They told me you are also
from Nigeria? You don't sound it."

"I've been here since I was six, I hope you don't
think I should have kept my accent that long."

He flinched at her rudeness but pressed on.

"I don't know many Nigerians here, maybe you can introduce me?"

Glory considered the handful of women she kept in touch with who would have *loved* to be introduced to this guy, still green and fresh. But they saw little of her real life, thinking Glory to be an ad exec with a fabulous lifestyle, and any introductions would jeopardize that.

"Sorry, I don't really know anyone either. You should try talking to someone with real friends."

He laughed, thinking she was joking, and his misunderstanding loosened her tongue. It was nice to talk to someone new who had no expectations of her.

"So, why are you slumming it here with the rest of us? Shouldn't you be interning somewhere fabulous?"

"This *is* my internship. I actually work in corporate but thought I should get a better understanding of what happens in the trenches."

"Wait, you're here voluntarily? Are you crazy?"

He laughed again. "No, it's just . . . you wouldn't understand."

"I'm not stupid," Glory said. "So fuck you." Then she switched on her headset, ignoring his "Whoa, where did that come from?," and turned her dial to the busiest queue. The calls came in one after the other, leaving Thomas little chance to apologize if he wanted to.

An hour in, he pressed a note into Glory's palm. *I'm sorry*, it read. *Can I treat you to lunch?*

Her pride said no, but her stomach, last filled with the sandwich she'd stolen yesterday afternoon, begged a yes.

She snatched up his pen. *I guess.*

M*om, I'm seeing someone.* Glory typed and deleted that sentence over and over, never sending it. Her mother would call for sure, and then she'd dissect every description of Thomas till he was flayed to her satisfaction. Her father would ask to hear the "young man's intentions." The cloying quality of their attention would ruin it.

Thomas would have delighted them. He went to church every Sunday—though he'd learned to stop inviting her—and he had the bright sort of future that was every parent's dream. He prayed over his meals, and before he went to bed, and when he woke up. He prayed for her.

Glory despised him. She hated the sheen of accomplishment he wore, so dulled on her. She hated his frugal management of money. She hated that when she'd pressed him for sex he'd demurred, saying that they should wait till they were more serious.

Glory couldn't get enough of him. She loved that he watched Cartoon Network with the glee of a teenager, loved that he could move through a crowd of strangers and emerge on the other side with friends. He didn't seem to mind her coarseness, or how her bad luck had deepened her bitterness so that she wished even the best of people ill. He didn't seem to mind how joy had become a finite meal she begrudged seeing anyone but herself consume. She wanted to ask him what he saw in her but was afraid his answer would be qualities she knew to be illusions. A carefree attitude that was simply carelessness. Bluntness mistaken for honesty when she was just mean.

They talked of Nigeria often, or at least he did, telling her about growing up in Onitsha and how he wanted to move back someday. He said *we* and *us* like it was understood she'd go back with him, and she began to savor a future she'd never imagined for herself.

She'd been to Nigeria many times, in fact, but she kept that from him, enjoying, then loathing, then enjoying how excited he was to explain the country to her. He didn't know that what little money she could scrape together was spent on a plane ticket to Nigeria every thirteen months, or that over the past few years, she had arrived the day after her grandmother's death, then the day after her great-aunt's death, and then her uncle's, so that her grandfather asked her to let him know when she booked her ticket so that he could prepare to die. Thomas still didn't know she was unlucky.

She kept it secret to dissuade any probing, unaware that people like Thomas were never suspicious, as trusting of the world's goodness as children born to wealth. When she visited her grandfather, they'd sit together in his room watching TV, Glory getting up only to fetch them food or drink. Nobody knew why she made the trips as often as she did, or why she eschewed the bustle of Lagos for her grandfather's sleepy village. She couldn't explain that her grandfather knew her, saw her for what she was—a black hole that compressed and eliminated fortune and joy—and still opened his home to her, gave her a room and a bed, the mattress so old the underside bore stains from when her mother's water broke.

Near the end of her last stay, their conversation had migrated to her fate.

"There is only disaster in your future if you do not please the gods," he'd said.

The older she got, the more she felt the truth of it: the deep inhale her life had been so far, in preparation for an explosive exhale that would flatten her.

"Papa, you know I don't have it in me to win anyone's favor, let alone the gods'."

They were both dressed in shorts and singlets, the voltage of the generator too low to carry anything that cooled. Glory sat on the floor, shifting every half hour to savor the chill of cooler tiles. Her grandfather lounged on the bed. When he began one of his fables, she closed her eyes.

"A porcupine and a tortoise came to a crossroads, where a spirit appeared before them. 'Carry me to the heart of the river and let me drink,' the spirit said. Neither wanted to be saddled with the spirit, but they could not deny it without good reason.

"'I am slow,' said the tortoise, 'it will take us many years to reach the river.'

"'I am prickly,' said the porcupine, 'the journey will be too painful.'

"The spirit raged. 'If you don't get me to the heart of the river by nightfall and give me a cup to drink, I will extinguish every creature of your kind.'

"The tortoise and the porcupine conferred. 'What if you carry me,' said the tortoise, 'while I carry the spirit? We will surely make it by nightfall.'

"'I have a better idea,' said the porcupine. 'These are no ordinary quills on my back. They are magic quills capable of granting any wish. The only condition is that you must close your eyes and open them only after your wish is granted.'

"The tortoise and the spirit each plucked a quill, eager for desires out of reach, and closed their eyes. That's when the porcupine snatched the quill from the tortoise and jammed it into the flesh of his throat. He filled the spirit's hands with the tortoise's blood, which it drank, thinking the gurgling it heard to be from the river. But spirits know the taste of blood. It lashed out at the porcupine, only to find that it could move no faster than a tortoise. The porcupine continued on his way."

Her grandfather's long pause signaled the end.

"Are you hearing me?"

"Yes, but what does it mean?"

"If you can't please the gods, trick them."

Glory's time with her grandfather had eased the pressure building in her, but the relief had been short-lived. A stream of catastrophes greeted her stateside: Keys left on the plane. A car accident, her foot slipping on the pedal made smooth by the car insurance check she'd forgotten to mail. A job lost for lack of transportation, which after many fruitless applications had landed her in the petri dish of the call center where she'd met Thomas.

Thomas, on the other hand, was a lucky man. He always seemed to find money lying about the street, although never so large an amount as to induce alarm or guilt. He always got what he wanted, always, and attributed it to ingenuity and perseverance, unaware of the halo of good fortune resting on his head. When Glory had him write a new request to Facebook, her page was restored in a day. He would have been appalled to know she sometimes followed him when they parted ways after work, watching with fascination as he drew amity from everyone he encountered.

Some of his luck did rub off on her and she found herself receiving invitations to long-standing events she hadn't even known existed. Igbo Women's Fellowship of the Midwest. Daughters of Biafra, Minnesota chapter. Party, Party, a monthly event rotated among different homes. Sometimes, as she watched Thomas charm a crowd with little effort, she wondered how it was that one person could be so blessed and another not. They'd been born in the same state to parents of similar means and faith. Even accounting for the privileges of his maleness, it seemed to Glory that they should have been in the same place. She began to think of his luck as something that had been taken from her and viewed their relationship as a way to even her odds.

At last they were serious enough for Thomas, and the sex was not mediocre exactly, but just good, not the mind-blowing experience she'd expected it to be. But Thomas was moved and thanked her for trusting him, and she said, "You're welcome," in that cutesy, girlish way she knew he would like, even though what she really wanted was for him to stop being such a gentleman and fuck her silly.

And the more he said *us* and *we*, the less quickly she deleted that *Mom, I'm seeing someone* text. One day, instead of sending it, she posted a picture of her and Thomas on her Facebook wall, setting off a sequence that involved her Port Harcourt cousin calling another cousin who called another and so on and so forth, until the news reached her mother, who called her. It took thirty-seven minutes.

Glory waited till just before the call went to voice mail to pick up.

"Hello?"

"Who is he? Praise God! What is his name?"

"Thomas Okongwu," and at *Okongwu* her mother started praising God again. Glory couldn't help but laugh and felt a blush of gratitude. It had been years since any news she'd delivered over the phone had given her mother cause for joy. She told her about Thomas and his ambitions, getting more animated the more excited her mother became. She ignored the undercurrent of disbelief on the other end of the line, as if her mother couldn't quite believe her daughter had gotten something right.

After that, it was like everything she did was right. Her job, long pilloried, was now a good thing. The fact that she had no career, her father wrote, meant that she could fully concentrate on her children when they came along. Her ineptitude at managing money no longer mattered. You see, he continued, she'd picked the perfect man to make up for her weaknesses. Kind where she was not, frugal where she was not. Successful.

Glory stared at her father's e-mail, meant to comfort but instead bringing to mind the wine and pills and what they could do to a body. She moved the message to a folder she'd long ago titled "EVIDENCE"—documents gathered to make her case if she chose never to speak to her father again.

When Thomas asked her if she'd like to meet his mother, Glory knew the right answer and gave it. But she panicked at the prospect of having to impress this woman. Her parents had been easy. Thomas was impressive. She was not.

"Why do you want me to meet her?" she asked. She knew the question was a bit coy, but she wanted some reassurance to hold on to.

Thomas shrugged. "She asked to meet you."

"So you didn't ask her if she wanted to meet me?"

After a patient rolling of eyes, Thomas gripped her shoulders and shook her with gentle exasperation.

"You're always doing this. Of course I want you to meet her and of course she wants to meet you. You're all she ever talks about now. Look." He dialed his cell phone. Glory heard a woman laugh on the other end of the line and say something that made Thomas laugh too. Then he said, "Hey, Mum, she's right here. I'll let you talk, but don't go scaring her off." The warm phone was pressed to her ear, and a voice just shy of being too deep for a woman's greeted her.

Glory tried to say all the right things about herself and her family, which meant not saying much about herself at all. She wanted this woman to like her, and even beyond that, to admire her, something she wasn't sure she could achieve without lies. On Facebook, she'd pretended to quit her job at the ad firm—a "sad day indeed," an old college friend had written on her wall, making Glory suspect he knew the truth. (She unfriended him right away.) But Thomas's mother could not be so easily dismissed. Glory trotted out her parents' accomplishments—engineer mother, medical-supply-business-owner father—to shore up her pedigree. Then she mentioned more recent social interests of hers, like the Igbo women's group, leaving out Thomas's hand in that. All the while her inner voice wondered what the hell she was doing. *Tricking the gods*, she replied.

The day Thomas's mother flew in, Glory cooked for hours at his apartment. She'd solicited recipes from her mother, who took much joy in walking her through every step over the phone. By the time Thomas left for the airport, his apartment was as fragrant as a buka, with as large a variety of dishes awaiting eager bellies.

His mother was tall and Glory felt like a child next to her. His mother was also warm, and she folded Glory into a perfumed, bosomy hug.

"Welcome, ma," Glory said, then wanted to kick herself for sounding so deferential.

"My dear, no need to be so formal, I feel like I've known you for years, the way my son goes on and on. It's me who should be welcoming you into the family."

She complimented each dish, tasting a bit of one after the other and nodding before filling her plate. It was a test, and Glory was gratified to see that she had passed.

Thomas squeezed her leg under the table, a reassuring pressure that said, *See? Nothing to worry about.* But what did a person like him know about worry? When his mother questioned her about her work, it was clear she assumed Glory worked in corporate with Thomas, and neither of them dissuaded her. Yet it rankled Glory, who couldn't decide whether Thomas had stretched the truth into a more presentable form or hadn't realized what his mother would assume.

Thomas used the pause that followed to excuse himself on an errand. Glory, knowing there was no such errand, gripped his hand tight, pleading. Thomas pried his hand away while his mother busied herself adjusting her coffee to her liking.

He leaned over and whispered, "Just be you. She likes you already, relax."

Thomas pecked Glory on her nervous, trembling mouth and kissed his mother on the cheek. As soon as the door closed behind him, the older woman spoke.

"Well, it's just us girls now, what should we chat about?" She smiled an invitation at Glory, who took a long sip of water to mask her anxiety. When she didn't say anything, Thomas's mother took the lead.

"So you two are supervising a group of three hundred? You should have no problem with a family then. Thomas says they are like a bunch of unruly children." She laughed.

Glory knew she should laugh, too, make light of the notes posted around the call center asking people not to steal food. But her contrary nature stirred.

"Actually, I am one of those unruly children. I work the floor."

"Oh." Then seamlessly, "Well, it's no matter at this point, is it. I'm so happy that you will soon leave the US to come and stay with me in Nigeria. It's so important to bring up the children there. Thomas's father and I are delighted that you both agree."

This was something Glory and Thomas had never discussed. If he'd been there, he would have squeezed her leg, a silent *Please don't argue with my mother.* Glory felt it then, that peculiar knot at the back of her neck that tensed whenever she came to a crossroads. The prospect of disappointing Thomas so boldly was the only thing that stayed her tongue. Unfortunately, that reticence extended to the rest of their exchange.

"So, no siblings."

"No."

"You didn't enjoy that, I'm sure. Kids need companions, don't you think?"

"I guess."

Every minute that passed without Thomas by her side, Glory felt as though a veil was slipping off her, revealing more and more of her true nature. With every question his mother asked, and every terse answer she gave, Glory felt his mother close off a bit, leaning back as though to consider what manner of girl she was. Her interior was frantic, grasping for something interesting to say, but monosyllables were all she could manage.

After thirty minutes, his mother's pleasantness had cooled to politeness and Glory excused herself to the bathroom before it chilled further.

You have to come back now, she texted Thomas. Now!

And he did, just as his mother grew serious and leaned in to have some say. Perfect timing as always. Always perfect.

With Thomas there, the ease between the two women returned, but the more they talked, the more his mother touched on the expectation that Glory would drop everything and go back to Nigeria and live there with her hypothetical children, in her mother-in-law's house. Thomas was most comfortable in Nigeria and would move back when he was done with schooling to join Glory, who would already be settled. If the idea had been hers, or if she'd even been asked, Glory might not have minded, but all this was delivered as a given, not a choice. All Thomas's talk of *we* and *us* felt less like a collaboration now and more like a general commanding his troops. It surprised Glory to realize that she had not been the only one scheming.

After they took his mother to her hotel, Thomas and Glory idled in the parking lot, each waiting for the other to break the silence. Then, offering neither apology nor explanation, Thomas placed a box on Glory's lap. She opened it, the hinge levering to reveal a ring that, just a year ago, she would never have imagined herself receiving. The tension returned to her neck.

A part of Glory had always thought to win her parents' good graces by her own merit. She held out hope that one day all her missteps would stumble her into accomplishments she could hold up as her own, that the seeming chaos of her life would coalesce into an intricate puzzle whose shape one could see only when it was complete. That this ring was to be her salvation—she couldn't bear it. And yet, salvation it was. Acceptance into many proper folds. Lies she would never again have to tell. She could lose herself in the whirlwind of Thomas, golden child become golden man.

But then Glory thought back to that first time she'd turned her luck with a truly reckless move, the thing with the dog. There was her uncle's dog, napping. She'd felt antsy all over and a thought wormed into her head, that the tension would go away if she touched the dog's tongue. It suddenly seemed the right and only thing to do. She rubbed the scar now, thinking of all the times she'd picked stupid over sensible, knowing, just knowing, that this time she'd gotten it right. She could not afford to get it wrong again.

Looking at the ring, resentment and elation warred till one overcame the other and Glory made another decision.

WHAT IS A VOLCANO?

▲ ▼ ▲

The god of ants and the goddess of rivers were feud-
ing. Their feud was in the early stages, more a
cause for rolled eyes and snickers than alarm. River
had divided one of her streams, and the new current
washed away a small anthill of no real consequence,
except Ant had grown especially fond of this fledgling
colony. He complained first to the goddess of hearts,
legendary for her sympathy. Then to the god of vengeance, known for his, well, vengeance. Ant approached
many other deities, trying to talk them onto his side of
things, but those who did not smite him simply
laughed, for Ant was the most minor of the gods,
hardly more than a spirit, and who even knew there
was a god of ants, did you?

So Ant began to exact his revenge in little ways, dumping mounds of dirt into small waters so that they sludged and ran slow. River retaliated by overflowing the banks Ant scouted for his colonies, rendering the once-dry shores too wet to build anything of use. Ant then had his minions shred the reeds that stemmed the tide in a small village, so that the waters ran into the crops and the angry famers cursed the river.

They backed and forthed for five human centuries, and if anyone asked River what she thought of Ant, she responded with an affectionate laugh peppered with annoyance. Such a small man with small concerns, but a fun diversion for such a woman as she. No one asked Ant what he thought of River, but someone should have known that you do not take small things from small men. Ant loathed River. He hated the condescending laugh she gave when his name was mentioned. He hated that she seemed to take pleasure in finding the tiny colonies he'd squirreled by a lake or stream. One day, he came upon the washed-out remains of one such colony, the queen mired in mud, undignified, laid bare for anyone to see. So mighty was River, so respected and loved and worshipped. What were ants to her? He decided to show River what it felt like to lose.

The mightiest river, from which all rivers flowed, was the source of River's power. Ant sent one ant with one stone into the stillest, deepest part. Then he sent another. And another. At first, the stones just added a nice pebbled finish to the bed of the river. But over a thousand years, the stones began to amass.

River's new twins distracted her or she would have noticed the change in current sooner. But for now, they were delightful girls whose eyes followed her and her alone. So rare was the birth of god-twins that they drew a steady stream of visitors bearing tribute and admiration. Two firstborn, how marvelous. They would become the most powerful river goddesses the world had ever seen. When the flow of guests finally abated, River noticed the waning of her power, too much to be the result of the birth, from which she had long since recovered. Leaving her daughters in the care of her sister, she walked the bank. When she got to the site of Ant's not-quite-finished dam, she pushed a wave at it, not knowing its cause or the resentment that cemented it. The stone wall repelled the wave, so powerfully that it knocked her over. Ant, who had been in the process of adding more stones, laughed and laughed, but silently, so he did not give away his hiding place. See River, knocked to the ground by the forces she controlled!

The problem with those who don't know real power is that they do not know real power. River pushed again with all her rage, and this time the wall gave, the force of the water so great that it burst over the dam and flooded half the world. And in this half of the world was the largest ant colony you can imagine, a maze created over generations, a honeycomb of earth piled into a mountain so high that even the god of mountains was forced to respect it. But River's fury washed it away.

Seeing this, Ant lost all reason. He ran to River's house and, while her sister slept, slipped through an open window and snatched the children. He hid one girl in a colony of army ants, ordering them to guard the child from anyone who would take her, and the other he hid in a location where River would never think to look.

Unaware that her daughters had been taken, River dealt instead with the other gods and goddesses whose dwelling places were flooded. The god of birds had lost a quarter of his flock when they tired with no place to land. She begged forgiveness and they gave it easily, because was this not our River, so known to us, and had she not just birthed the next generation of gods?

The wail alerted her. So much anguish in that wail. River rushed back to her house, hoping the familiar voice or its anguish was simply a trick in her ear. But there was her sister, ripping her hair out by the roots, and there was the empty crib, barely cooled of the warmth of her girls. River released a tsunami of sound, and every god that could walk or fly, every spirit that haunted every place, came to her. Who, she wanted to know, and where? No one could think of anyone who would wish River such harm. Even Death shrugged his innocence, he who had taken something from everyone present. River's sister hadn't seen or heard anything, lost as she had been in the sweetest of sleeps. No one said it, but they all thought, *This is what you get for asking a godling to do the work of a god.* None of them, not even Love, kept in contact with their half-divine siblings, lest they discover that by putting the most powerful of their bloodline to rest, they might graduate to godhood themselves. Poor River, so indulgent, so generous, and look how she had been repaid.

The other gods prepared to smite her sister, and River was scared by the emptiness inside her where loyalty should lie. Then a field spirit stepped forward, terrified but determined, and held up a fragment of the dam for everyone to see. Ants. It was ants that held the wall together, and resentment that gave them the power.

River didn't want to believe it. Ant was responsible? The little god with whom she'd traded pranks for millennia? Rage replaced disbelief, and River went hunting.

If Ant had stuck around when he'd dropped the first girl with the army ants, he could have prevented the scene to which he returned. If he'd stuck around, he would have noticed that the loss of the ancestral ant colony lessened his ant-controlling powers. He would have seen the ants swarm the child the moment he turned away, so eager for the taste of god-flesh. What many don't know, a secret god-mothers have kept for eternity, is that god-children are just that, children. And just as a human child must learn to talk and to walk and to join the world of their parents, so must a god-child learn to become a deity. But unlike human children, god-children must even learn to grow, guided by their mothers from one stage to the next until they attain godhood. River's child was too young to know she was divine and could not be eaten, and so she was. Ant returned to shards of bone, picked clean of marrow. He heard his name being screamed across the world and he knew River could never, ever know. She would drown the universe.

Ant ground the girl's bones to dust and compacted it with panic and regret into a small blue stone. Into the stone he whispered the location of the dead girl's sister, then deleted it from his memory. Such knowledge was too dangerous to have in these times. Then he went into hiding among the humans, trying to live as one of them. He married human women who bore children he suffocated as they slept, lest they leave a divine trail that led to his end. When the women grew suspicious, he abandoned them, and they would go mad or move on with their lives, slowly forgetting him as one does a god who answers no prayers.

River searched the world for her girls. She dug up every anthill she could find. The army ants were too frightened to tell her what they'd done, but they did tell her that the ant god had gone to live among the humans. River searched for Ant. She dug through entire lineages trying to find him. When, after three hundred years, the sky god dared to mention the neglected waters of the world, she dried up entire countries out of spite. This is our River, one god reminded the other, our sweet River. Let us help, not hinder. And so they sent emissaries from every spirit realm, second daughters and minor spirits of similar powers, godlings all, promising their aid for a hundred years. But River's grief was so deep it consumed them, and her grief became their own. They forgot their mothers and their brothers and the lovers they'd promised to return to; they forgot that they'd had a past before this grief removed everything from inside of them. How, they wondered, can a body feel full to bursting with grief but also hollow? These godlings of land and air and memory resisted this loss of themselves, but River's sorrow drowned them. Their husbands, their children, their homes became like reflections in a rough stream, fractured beyond recognition.

They tore the world apart. Unprecedented rains. Earthquakes that ravaged every region. One godling who had come from the house of flames set an entire city on fire trying to find River's girls. It was a dark century for humankind and godkind alike. Then the female godlings got craftier in their search. They made themselves visible to human eyes, tempting men and women, threatening men and women, building a network of spies across the globe who lit candles and prayed to them and passed this new religion on to their children. Every new convert was a new set of eyes in the world, a new set of ears to catch whispers of men who didn't seem to fit in, or men who rose to ungodly success but never seemed to pray. Many a good man was lost to angry godlings who peeled his skin away, searching for the god that might be hidden inside.

But after seven hundred fruitless years and countless human believers in her service, it dawned on River that she might never see her twins again. She collapsed where she stood, and every emissary lay down as well. Dust settled on them, then grime and so much debris that they became part of the earth, hills of hips and buttocks and woe.

All but one. The only one who felt the rage of River, multiplied by that most powerful feeling that won't let a person rest: guilt. River's sister, not quite goddess. The guilt turned in her belly like a ship in a storm. She'd slept while her sister's children were taken. Blame, so like a god itself, shadowed her, occupied her bed like a lover, whispered to her like a dearest friend. Her name was eventually forgotten. Soon all called her She Who Betrayed River, a name that over the years degenerated to Betrayed River, then Bereaver, which stuck, and eventually even Bereaver forgot she had ever been anyone else. Guilt crushed every milestone in her life to dust so that she knew only Before and After. And Before seemed like the unfathomable dream of a foolish woman.

Long after River and her women collapsed, Bereaver searched alone, turning every crust of earth to
find Ant and her nieces. Whenever a kind wind caught
a whisper and blew Ant's name into her ear, she would
follow it to the city, town, village to which he had run
and pluck the man, woman, child who had seen him
last. She pulled every secret from them, things they
didn't even know they knew, and afterward she'd pull
out their eyes, tongue, heart, so they'd never know a
thing again. Sometimes she just missed him. Other
times, the trail was so stale it crumbled to nothing
when she walked it, the people who had known the
human Ant long dead.

Ant tried to live quiet lives, but eventually someone would sense something about him, be it his wick-
edness or his divinity, and he would be run out of
town—or become so highly acclaimed he feared catching the attention of a god who would recognize him.
Much as it galled him, he knew he would have to set
his godhood aside if he wanted to keep his life. He
would also have to separate himself from the stone
that held his secrets.

So into the stone Ant whispered everything he'd
ever been and sealed it with the human name he'd
taken for this earth. He kept only his immortality, so

that he could one day live to be restored, no longer hunted. He tried to bury the stone, but animals circled the spot and began to dig. He gave it to a boy, but the boy ran to show his friends, so Ant snatched it back and buried the boy instead. In his despair, he carved a cave into a hill and thought to hide there for eternity. He pulled in a large rock and made it his bed, as penance. But a hundred years went by and he became bored with piety and regret. Poking his head out of the cave, he saw a girl hauling a pail of water. The water wasn't hers, he was sure, and yet she bore it on her head with grace and little complaint. He watched her for days, carrying water back and forth, back and forth, but for whom? To do what? Boys sometimes danced around her, trying to distract her from her task, but on she went, day after day. It dawned on Ant then that one could ask almost anything of a girl. He stepped out of the cave to block her path and, holding out the pretty blue stone, said, Can you keep a secret?

The girl took the stone, so accepting that it sank into her palm, lodging itself at the base of her fingers. She was filled with a terrifying knowledge—a child bled to bones, a mother who thought it alive and well—and certainty that she must never, ever tell.

So Bereaver still wanders, not knowing that Ant is

lost to her. The girl will carry his secret, and when she is no longer a girl, she will give it to another girl, and this sorrow stone will be stolen away in uniform pockets and hidden under the pillows of marriage beds, secreted in diaries, guarded closely by the type of girls who, above all else, obey.

And while Bereaver wanders, River and her women lie catatonic with heartache, dreaming of their children. And when, in the place she is hidden, the surviving god-child cries, their bodies hear her, and their breasts weep, and that, since you asked, is a volcano.

REDEMPTION

▲ ▼ ▲

The day after we met, she sent a missile of shit wrapped in newspaper like a gift. It exploded on the side of the house, scattering chunks and leaving a streak of brown. My mother, furious, railed about the neighbors (never at them, mind you) and lamented that they just didn't make house girls like they used to. I, on the other hand, fell in love.

Mayowa was thirteen going on whatever age it is that women find themselves. Mr. and Mrs. Ajayi took her on to replace Abigail, who had worked for them as long as we'd lived next door. My mother said it was about time, a woman that old should be the madam of her own house, not cleaning up someone else's.

"They need an energetic young thing, but not one of those ambitious ones. They never last long." Mother recited the virtues of young workers nonstop— malleable, easily intimidated, unlikely to seduce the man of the house or turn up pregnant. Then she met the young worker in question. The Ajayis had brought Mayowa over to get us used to seeing her. Prodded by Mrs. Ajayi, she curtsied stiffly to my mother, as though her knees rebelled. My mother noticed.

"And this is the young madam," Mrs. Ajayi teased at me, and Mayowa's curtsy was even more reluctant. Understandable, as we were the same age, but my mother wasn't having it.

"See this one. Nancy, you are going to have trouble with her," my mother said, adding, "You are too kind," when Mrs. Ajayi explained that Mayowa was the child of a third cousin who couldn't afford to send her to school. As though to confirm my mother's predictions, Mayowa raised her bowed head and met my mother's eyes straight on.

"So bold. And look at that." She waved a hand to indicate Mayowa's backside. Mayowa was small for her age, with a compact muscular frame that promised to blossom into something interesting.

"This one will be bringing boys around soon, if she

hasn't started already," my mother said, calling Mayowa's virtue into question. The answer arrived the next
day, wrapped in the contested results of last week's
election.

Grace, our house girl, who had to clean up the
mess, took to sneering whenever she saw Mayowa or
heard her name. Grace was nineteen, far older than
what my mother considered prime house girl age, and
prettier than my mother would have liked, but my
father was long gone, so she kept her. When anyone
asked where my father was, my mother would say he
was traveling, which was true if *traveling* meant "I pre-
fer my mistress's cooking, so I'm going to live with
her now."

I began to spend most of my time outside, knocking
lemons out of the tree, swirling the dirt on my mother's car, shading with the lizards. When the Ajayis'
gate creaked, I'd run to our gate and peek through a
crack in the metal. Sometimes it was the husband or
wife leaving, sometimes it was the man who cared
for their dogs, but most of the time it was Mayowa,
strutting on her way to school or the market or just
down the road to the pharmacy. She walked as though

WHAT IT MEANS WHEN A MAN FALLS FROM THE SKY

the earth spun to match her gait. I liked to think that if she'd known I was there, she'd have turned around and waved.

Mrs. Ajayi was very old, creeping on that age when life begins to lose all meaning, fifty, I think. I would go and sit with her because everyone knows how old people enjoy the company of young people. They suck at us like vampires, or wilting flowers that require the sunshine of our youth. Whenever Mrs. Ajayi saw me she sighed, and it wasn't till I was much older that I realized it wasn't a sigh of relief.

She fed me Fanta and chinchin and listened to me talk and talk and talk. Sometimes, greased by loneliness, her secrets would slip out and she would mention things she shouldn't have, like how her oldest son couldn't find a job and how Mr. Ajayi was getting tired of lending him money. I was her young confidante, the daughter she never had, except for the two daughters she did have, who came by every few Sundays with their young children.

I wasn't worried about Mayowa replacing me. She wasn't the sort of girl who could sit and listen to old women and their problems. In fact, she seemed like the sort of girl who would hide an old woman's medication and watch the trembling in the woman's hands increase till she was too incapacitated to stop Mayowa from cleaning out her purse. I liked her a lot.

And so I stepped up my visits to Mrs. Ajayi, my sometimes biweekly calls multiplying to weekly, then near daily, as I found any reason to stop by.

"Mrs. Ajayi, my mother needs the pot she borrowed you six months ago."

"Mrs. Ajayi, can I have the ripe guava from your tree?"

"Mrs. Ajayi, there is a string hanging from my dress, can you fix it?"

And when she called Mayowa to fetch the pot or the scissors or the old mop handle to knock the tallest fruits, I stared, trying to figure out what aspect of this girl made her brave enough to throw shit at my mother. Her hair was cropped short, barely enough left to cover her scalp, and did nothing to enhance the squat ordinariness of her face. *That's all she is*, I told myself, *an ordinary girl*. And yet.

My visits to Mrs. Ajayi steadied at twice a week, once when Mayowa was there—I'd ask for something that needed fetching so I could watch her, study the boldness of her movements—and once when she wasn't, so Mrs. Ajayi could talk freely.

Mrs. Ajayi would ask after my mother and

sometimes, tentatively, my father, in between the recitation of her week so far and its most exciting aspects. This usually meant hearing about something Mayowa had done.

I picked these stories out of the trash of Mrs. Ajayi's boring day, her lazy son, Mr. Ajayi's intestinal distress. There was the time Mayowa held down one of the students at her school, pinned the girl's head between her knees, and scraped off half her cornrows with a razor blade before an adult intervened. And the day she taunted the dogs so much, leaving their bowls just out of reach, that they growled and bit their caretaker for the first time since they were untrained pups. Or how she served Mr. Ajayi far more meat than his old gut could handle, so she could feast on his leftovers. When I came across these morsels of Mayowa, I shelved them in my memory, where I could reimagine them over and over till I'd convinced myself I was there. I liked to think she would have wanted me to be.

Church meant my mother dressing me in frills too young for my years, sweating the starch out of said frills in the un-air-conditioned building, and seeing the woman my father left us for. She came every few

Sundays, when the weighty sin of fornicating with a married man became too heavy to bear. My mother didn't know that I knew who she was and understood why my mother never clapped when the woman gave a testimony of God's goodness. She always wore yellow, and she looked pretty in it. Not abandon-your-only-legitimate-child pretty, but you could see what a man would see in her. I imagined throwing something at her house, something hard, something that would hurt a man kissing her a distracted good-bye, his back turned so he doesn't see the rock sailing his way.

Brother Benni was the youth minister this week, and when they announced that the children should leave for Sunday school, I faked stomach pains to stay with my mother. She was annoyed and didn't hide it.

"You will stop with this Benni nonsense soon, he is a nice man."

And he was. After church, Brother Benni would mingle, bearing candies and biscuits, and the boys would mob him and snatch him bare in seconds. He'd lift the boys who could be lifted, roll them like barrels under his arms, and mock-stagger under their mock weight to the delight of almost all who watched. But the girls had learned to keep their distance.

Years ago, before my father left, when my mother

was a different person, I told her what Brother Benni had done to me. She went to my father, who went to the pastor, who went to Brother Benni, who called me a liar. That was the beginning of the end for us. The stink that was raised was what must have driven my father away, my mother occasionally reminded me. The humiliating stench of a daughter who bore false tales.

My mother was preening. Every third Sunday, a special offering was taken to support the Widows and Orphans Fund. And once in a while the pastor would give the week's donations, secured in a red velour bag with gold tassels, to a church member to take home and return the next week. It was a gesture of faith on the church's part and a testament to the trustworthiness of its members. This was the second time in a row my mother had gotten it and her sixth time overall. She was the most trusted woman in our church. She made sure everyone knew it.

"Six times, oh. Evelyn, you are the only one to beat me in this. Ah-ah, you've only had it four times? I forgot."

When she brought the bag home, she put it where

she always put it, on the shelf in the nice sitting room. If anyone stopped by during the week, they would see it on full display.

She made Grace dust around it and reminded her that "men want a trustworthy and godly woman. It is not just looks, you have to be honest and good." Grace, who had been on the receiving end of a few too many of my mother's corrective thrashings, pursed her lips and said nothing.

The next day, when my mother and Grace were at the market, Mayowa stopped by.

"Madam wants to know if your mummy has any lime."

My mother would have said no, even if we had, but I invited Mayowa inside while I checked. She hesitated at the back door, then stepped inside. She looked around the kitchen and I imagined her comparing it to the Ajayis'. It was larger but in poorer condition. Two cabinets were missing their doors, broken during one of my mother's rages. The door leading to the pantry was missing the handle. Bare concrete was visible in sections of the floor where the tiles were broken. It was a room that hadn't seen a man's handiwork in an age.

Wanting to impress Mayowa, I asked if she wanted

to see the rest of the house. She raised her brow, a gesture so like my mother's the hair on my arms prickled. My mother would have fainted with shame if she saw me treating a house girl like a guest, so I rushed her through the house, pointing to this and that. In the nice sitting room Mayowa stopped by the offering bag and, already more comfortable in my own house than I was, picked it up. Her eyes bulged at the roll of money inside.

"It's from the church," I explained, oddly proud for the first time. "They gave it to us to keep."

Mayowa put the bag down and I led her to the next room.

When we got to my bedroom, I pulled out the stack of old magazines I reread every few weeks. The covers were wrinkled and on the verge of losing their gloss. After my father left, we stopped buying magazines, the once-commonplace purchase now a luxury. I picked out my favorite one, a fashion magazine with pages and pages of women dressed in custom aseobi, and Mayowa and I fell into a silence as we envied the styles we were too young to wear. If she felt the sheet of protective plastic crinkle when she shifted on the bed, she chose to say nothing. I tried to even my breathing and silence the rapid thudding in my chest.

When I took a breath, I smelled the soap she used to wash her hair (disproving my mother's assertion that all village girls are dirty) and the muddy scent of yams she must have chopped earlier in the day. I wanted to know what she was thinking, if she found me as interesting as I found her, if she was as drawn to me as I was to her. If she wanted to be my friend.

I flipped the page and Mayowa pointed at a woman wearing a red-and-orange dress with too many frills and a train that belonged on a different dress. The image was circled with a pen and the page dog-eared.

"I like this one," she said.

I didn't. It was one my mother had circled a million years ago for our seamstress to make, back when she regularly had dresses made. It was ugly, something Grace and I agreed on, and my mother had overheard. The tongue-lashing Grace received had not been pretty. But Mayowa didn't know that. I hoped she thought I had circled it and said she liked it because she thought I liked it. I found myself wanting to tell her everything that had happened to me, why I started wetting the bed and why my father left. How Brother Benni had fisted my hair so tightly braids popped off my temple, leaving a bald spot that gleamed in certain lights.

The familiar sound of my mother's car horn honked

at the gate. I jumped up and scrambled to put the magazines away. Mayowa got up unhurriedly, still holding the magazine with the dress.

"You can keep it," I said, part kindness, part wanting to hustle her outside before my mother found her in the house. She nodded, unaffected by my mother's now-insistent honking.

I opened the gate and after my mother drove in, Mayowa snuck out, the magazine rolled in her fist.

The next day when I heard the Ajayis' gate squeak, I peered through our gate to see Mayowa holding a plastic bag that looked to be filled with empty bottles of Mr. Ajayi's prescriptions. She was going to the pharmacy, about a ten-minute walk within the estate. I must have made a noise, or she must have sensed me, because she stopped and stared in my direction, waiting. I lifted the metal lever that secured our gate and stepped out. She smiled the careful smile of one who hasn't much cause to. We matched gaits toward the pharmacy, neither of us speaking. While I tried to think of what to say, Mayowa quickened her steps and I sped to keep up. When she moved even faster, I kept pace. One of us giggled and we broke into a run at the same time, gasping and laughing. I made it to the store first. I liked to think she let me win.

I imagined how we would become good friends, how our secret friendship would come to define us over the years. We could run away and become Nollywood stars and live in an exclusive apartment on Victoria Island, like sisters, or something more, something I didn't yet have words for. I wanted her to teach me to throw things.

Mayowa and Grace were planning something. I could tell by the way they avoided each other's gaze and how whenever anyone called their names, they stilled like deer. My mother remained oblivious, except to note that Grace was getting clumsy and didn't she know that nobody wants a clumsy wife. "You would know," Grace muttered out of her hearing, and dared me with her gaze to tell. I tried to catch Mayowa's eye and whenever I did, I smiled tentatively, and she'd smile tentatively in return. But she didn't let me in on it, though I could have guessed.

I didn't say a word when I saw Grace eyeing the red velour bag. I didn't say a word when Mayowa, who was rarely at our house, invented reasons to stop by. Mother was not as kind to her as Mrs. Ajayi was to me, making her wait outside by the kitchen door for whatever it was she wanted. That's where she and Grace were talking when I heard "offering *mutter mutter* we can take transport *mutter mutter.*" I knew I should say something, but I didn't.

They were caught anyway. Grace's fault, I can imagine. They'd gotten as far as the bus station one town away, where they had planned to split up. Grace was returned to my mother in tears. Mayowa had melted into the crowd. The money disappeared, probably pocketed by the men who apprehended them. Grace's mother came up from the village to beg on her daughter's behalf. My mother wanted the full story, but every time Grace began with "Mayowa told me to—" my mother cut her off.

"How can some little girl tell you what to do? You will tell me the truth now. If you do not tell the truth, I will take you to the police. Do you want to go to the police?" Everybody knew what happened to pretty young girls in police stations.

The new truth made Grace the mastermind. She'd planned the robbery from beginning to end and roped Mayowa in because she was young and followed orders. That didn't sound right to me and couldn't have sounded right to my mother, but there was something between the two women my mother had finally won.

Mayowa showed up three days later, dirty and hungry but unharmed. Mrs. Ajayi, who didn't believe her innocent any more than I did, hesitated to let her in but didn't have it in her to turn away a child at her gate. A strange mood permeated our corner of the estate.

Mayowa ambushed me the next day, as I walked past the Ajayis' gate to our own.

"You told."

"No, I—"

"You told." She sneered and spat on the ground.

I wanted to tell her I would never, and that she even thought I would stung me. I wanted to tell her that the next time she wanted to run, I would run with her. The weight of all I wanted to tell her sat in my mouth and stilled my tongue.

She ignored me from then on. When I stopped by the Ajayis' she found ways to not be around, and when it was unavoidable she kept her attention on Mrs. Ajayi and never looked my way.

I felt jilted, and in that sly way infatuation can flip, the turning over of a mattress to hide an embarrassing stain, I began to despise her. I thought of Grace and

WHAT IT MEANS WHEN A MAN FALLS FROM THE SKY

her beating, the many ways a girl can be broken. And
I began to lie.

"Mrs. Ajayi, Mayowa told me she kept some of the
change when she went to the market."

"Mrs. Ajayi, Mayowa complained you haven't been
feeding her, is that true?"

"Mrs. Ajayi, Mayowa said she preferred feeding the
dogs living outside to the ones living inside, whatever
did she mean?"

I wanted the Ajayis to beat her, to open her up and
scoop out the thing that made her brave. To leave her
like the rest of us, like me.

They sent her to Brother Benni. For deliverance,
Mrs. Ajayi told my mother. He was so good with children and Mayowa was a troubled child in need of
prayer. Mrs. Ajayi was shocked at what followed.

What followed: Brother Benni was praying with
the girl in his office when he began to howl and howl.
It was a Wednesday night and the people attending
Bible study rushed to see the fuss.

What followed: Brother Benni crouched on the
floor, gripping his upper thigh around a flowing
wound. Several someones called on the name of Jesus.
Someone called for a car so they could take him to the
hospital. Someone grabbed Mayowa and squeezed her

wrist till she dropped the razor blade. Someone asked what they were to do with this mad girl. It was Mrs. Ajayi who got the story from her, about how Brother Benni pulled out his oko and tried to make her taste it. It was Mrs. Ajayi who overrode the protests of the crowd by pointing out that Brother Benni's belt was unbuckled and asking why, if Mayowa cut his leg for no reason, was there no matching tear on his trouser. Someone called the police despite Brother Benni's claim that the devil made him do it. Someone said it's not like he did anything, the girl stopped him, no need to call the authorities for a crime that never happened. Nobody bothered calling off the police, who would arrive long after the church was vacant.

It was settled. Brother Benni would go to the hospital and Mayowa would go away. For her own protection, Mrs. Ajayi said. You know how people can be about these things.

What followed: my mother, fist strangling the arm of the settee, face like a stone.

I ran from the house to the Ajayis' gate, grateful to find it unlatched. The man who watched the dogs waved a lazy hand my way as I zoomed past him. I knew I was breaking some rule by being there without Mrs. Ajayi to watch or welcome me, but I had to see Mayowa.

I found her in the kitchen, scrubbing the floor so spitefully it might have been punishment in addition to chore. She spat on the tile and ground it into the grout like she was laying a curse on the foundation of the house. She hadn't yet noticed me and I stepped back to watch her for a while. After a few minutes of angry, frantic scrubbing, her arms began to falter and she leaned back on her haunches, swiping the sweat off her face with the hem of her dress. No, not sweat. She continued to clean, sucking the tears into her mouth when she tasted salt. I backed away even further, knowing this wasn't something she'd want me to see.

She wasn't my friend. She wasn't here to fight for me. Or love me. She was just as powerless, another daughter being sent back to her mother in disgrace. My thanks felt foolish under the glare of this truth. Girls with fire in their bellies will be forced to drink from a well of correction till the flames die out.

But my tongue stirred anyway. I stepped into view and threw something of my own.

ACKNOWLEDGMENTS

▲ ▼ ▲

I am greatly indebted to:

My parents, Chris and Ify Arimah, for surviving my teen years and producing such a lovely young(ish) woman.

My siblings, Stanley, Shirley, Ronald, and Roland— co-conspirators, enablers of my better parts.

My writing group, Jen, Jason, Ruby, and Romelle. This book would not have come together as it did without you—a toast to accountability.

My Minneapolis crew, Shevvi, Erin, Adeya, Mawusi, and Bianca. You have no idea how many times you saved me.

My Vona '13 "Bakers Dozen"—Christine, Glendaliz, Junot, Kai, Kiran, Lesley, Leticia, Miguel,

Rois, Sepeyeonkqua, Sharline, and Yalitza. I can point to this moment in time as when I learned what it means to write fearlessly. Thank you for helping me grow.

Brandy Colbert, who knows the journey it took to get here. How lovely it is to still know you after all this time.

Diana Joseph, whose mentee I somehow (probably through nefarious means) became. Thank you for your sage, and unsage, advice.

Rebecca and Mary, for the unwavering friendship; the many nights writing around your dining table; the vodka.

My wonderful, wonderful agent, Samantha Shea, at Georges Borchardt, Inc.

My editor, Becky Saletan, and the Riverhead army. I am happy to be in your ranks.

Thank you all.